UNHOLY TRINITY

An Inspector Faro Mystery

Alanna Knight

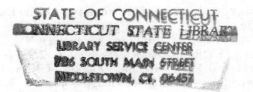

CHIVERS
THORNDIKE

This Large Print book is published by BBC Audiobooks Ltd, Bath, England and by Thorndike Press®, Waterville, Maine, USA.

Published in 2005 in the U.K. by arrangement with Black & White Publishing Ltd.

Published in 2005 in the U.S. by arrangement with Black & White Publishing Ltd.

U.K. Hardcover ISBN 1–4056–3179–1 (Chivers Large Print)
U.K. Softcover ISBN 1–4056–3180–5 (Camden Large Print)
U.S. Softcover ISBN 0–7862–7046–2 (General)

The text of this Large Print edition is unabridged.
Other aspects of the book may vary from the original edition.

Set in 16 pt. New Times Roman.

Printed in Great Britain on acid-free paper.

British Library Cataloguing in Publication Data available

Library of Congress Cataloging-in-Publication Data

Knight, Alanna.
    Unholy trinity : an Inspector Faro mystery / Alanna Knight.
      p.   cm.
    ISBN 0–7862–7046–2 (lg. print : sc : alk. paper)
    1. Faro, Jeremy (Fictitious character)—Fiction. 2. Ex-police officers—Fiction. 3. Scots—Ireland—Fiction. 4. Kerry (Ireland)—Fiction. 5. Weddings—Fiction. 6. Villages—Fiction. 7. Large type books. I. Title.

PR6061.N45U54 2005
813'.54—dc22   2004060643

For Helen and Charles Irvine with love

1

Murder was the last thing in Jeremy Faro's mind as the soft Irish countryside floated past the carriage window, partly obscured, for a moment, by the train's smoke, to emerge once again radiantly green. He smiled. This was Imogen's homeland. It unfurled in a glory of colour, a vast chequered quilt of variegated greens, yellows and browns, fields and mountains interrupted by glimpses of long fingers of land reaching out into fierce seas hurling white foam against the shore. Seas where islands lurked, mysterious shapes, holding their own against the elements, watching the land like basking primeval whales.

It was a land as fierce and proud as Imogen Crowe herself. Again he sighed. Soon they would be together again, but he was finding their separations harder and lengthier these days, as Imogen became more involved in researching a book on the life of the great Irish reformer and her personal hero, Daniel O'Connell. This was her reason for returning to Kerry from their travels in Europe.

As for Faro, for compensation and to keep him occupied, she had saddled him with a lecture tour in Dublin, Wexford and Cork which he completed last night. His final contribution had been a dry and (he thought) severely academic lecture on the crime methods of Edinburgh City Police, from which he had gladly retired a year ago, but talking about murder was not one of his favourite leisure activities. As a detective whose fame had spread far beyond the confines of Scotland, he was learning to evade invitations to speak which included lunch or dinner at eminent societies where, in addition to the notes he never used, he was unable to enjoy a glass of wine.

Sometimes, however, escape was impossible. His equivalent in the Irish Gardai in Dublin was an old colleague and it would have been churlish to refuse. Nevertheless, he hated giving talks, standing on a platform under the unflinching gaze of a sea of expressionless faces as he searched in vain for amusing anecdotes to lighten the atmosphere and bring a smile to their lips—such incidents were harder to find than clues to track down killers.

True, he had put up a firm resistance to the tour idea when it was originally suggested but then he had given in to Imogen's wheedling. 'Just a little favour.' 'Why,' she had said, 'wasn't the organiser a Dublin professor and fine poet, an old friend of her great uncle who had known Daniel O'Connell? So how could he, Jeremy Faro, the famous detective, ignore and refuse such an honour?' Besides, always

2

with a practical side, she had whispered that the fee was generous indeed, more than an advance for one of her books, and it would come in very useful for their further travels. 'Perhaps even New York. Think of that!' And, smiling sweetly, she had added, 'There is an alternative, of course.'

Faro recoiled even further from that particular alternative, an additional reason for this long-delayed and brief return to Kerry—the marriage of a distant but favourite cousin to whom she had promised, long ago in their childhood, that she would dance at her wedding. If anything, family weddings were more to be dreaded than murder lectures. Circumstances had conspired so that Faro should miss his two daughters' weddings—Emily's in Orkney and Rose's in America. And this particular family celebration in Carasheen would be his introduction to Imogen's vast, sprawling clan of relatives.

There would be another terrifying sea of faces, from the very old to the newest screaming arrival, all with impossible Gaelic names—Imogen, it seemed, was the one exception—names he would never remember or be able to pronounce correctly.

Shaking his head sadly, that other sea of unfamiliar scholarly faces he had just left was infinitely preferable, especially as he could already hear the Crowe clan's whispers across half of Kerry. Is that Imogen's man? And why then aren't they married? A widower, wasn't he? And her an auld spinster (a term applied to anyone over twenty-five). No just cause or impediment there. Faro shuddered as he imagined a more insensitive guest, emboldened by drink taken heartily, demanding, 'Sure now, and when is it yourself and Imogen are going to name the day?'

To say Imogen was neither mistress nor wife but described, by his family and, politely, by those who knew them both not too intimately, as his friend and travelling companion just wasn't a decent or satisfactory explanation for Imogen's marriage-orientated family.

Faro sighed more deeply than ever. Even in this enlightened year of 1890, mistresses were only for princes and aristocrats, the rich and the famous who could afford to flaunt convention with a defiant stare as they tore up the rules. Mistresses were not, definitely not, officially recognised by respectable Edinburgh and a whiff of such scandal had brought down many a promising career in the New Town.

Imogen's role in his life was not Faro's choice. He would have willingly slipped a ring on her finger any day of the week but she stubbornly declined the honour as an outrage to her firmly held feminist principles. Not that she didn't love Faro. She did. But a wedding ring signified the bondage she had scorned through her long career as a writer, defying convention, her main target women's rights and social injustices.

Truth to tell, as far as the British Government was concerned, Imogen Crowe was on record as an Irish terrorist who had spent time in a London jail. She had been wrongly accused, as it happened. Orphaned and sixteen years old, her uncle Brendan Crowe, a fanatical Irish patriot, had brought her to London where he secretly planned to assassinate Queen Victoria. The attempt failed and he had shot himself in their lodging. Imogen was taken prisoner as a suspect but ultimately proved innocent. However, even with her name cleared, she had assisted fellow countrymen to escape back to Ireland and, for that, she would be back behind bars if she ever set foot in Britain again. And it was this sad truth that also accounted for Faro's long exile from his family and friends.

Such were his thoughts as the train slowed down and slid along the platform at Carasheen station. Reeling down the window, he leaned out and there was Imogen staring anxiously at the carriage windows as they flashed past. Tall, slim, auburn-haired, white-skinned with black-lashed dark green eyes, that first sight of her, as always, was like a hammer blow to his chest. She was so lovely, the passing years took no toll. Touching forty, like Shakespeare's Cleopatra, age could not wither her nor custom stale her infinite variety. Faro smiled, priding himself for a moment that her eager, concerned expression hinted that she had missed him more severely than he dared hope in the two weeks they had been apart.

Gathering his luggage, he jumped out of the carriage. She ran towards him and, ready for that first embrace, he began, 'Well, how was the wed . . .' But he never finished the sentence.

Shaking her head impatiently, she seized his arm. 'Faro. Thank God you're here. Something absolutely dreadful has happened. There's been a murder—ten days ago, just after the wedding.' Before he could ask any questions she hurried through the gate, indicated the pony cart outside the station.

'I've put you in the local inn. I thought you would prefer that.' Faro didn't. He had been entertaining thoughts of a great bedroom, looking towards the sea, with a four-poster bed, snowy white sheets and Imogen's head on the pillow beside him.

She knew him well and, rightly interpreting his slight frown, she shook her head and said apologetically, 'Folk come a long way for family occasions like weddings, sleeping three and four to a room. All were so shocked by the killings of the Donnellys that they decided it was only proper and respectful to stay on for the funerals—and a wake.'

Shaking her head sadly, she added, 'Now they'll be inclined to stay until the whiskey runs out. No one in the Crowe family knows

6

the meaning of time.'

Aware of Faro's set expression, she grinned at him and squeezed his arm. 'Besides, I'm just fortunate to have a tiny room. Cousin Maeve's best friend died last month of consumption and she's nobly fostering four wee orphans. Very noisy. I couldn't inflict that on you, now could I?'

'Tell me about this murder,' was Faro's grumpy reply but he was aware that these were delaying tactics, that she was reluctant to talk about it.

Imogen shook her head, bewildered. 'The dancing and the drinking were in full swing—the bride and groom were off to Scotland to honeymoon. It was just before dawn and the effects of it all were beginning to slow the revellers down. Peg and Will Donnelly—recently married themselves—were on their way home, just a mile away, a little croft, and someone attacked them—took an axe . . .' Gulping, she closed her eyes, shutting out the scene. 'Dear God, it was terrible. Terrible.'

Faro seized the reins from her, 'Tell me later. Now, which way?'

Imogen's hands ceased their trembling. 'I'll be fine,' she said firmly, 'and I've put a picnic in the back. Thought we might have a few hours on our own.'

'What about the inn? Surely . . . ?' said Faro, thinking of that bedroom waiting for him.

Her reply was given with a sad, mocking

7

smile. 'Sure, that would be fine and dandy, wouldn't it, now? But the inn's packed too, crawling with Crowe kin. And they would only talk about us, wouldn't they?'

Faro considered. At that moment, longing for Imogen, he would have faced and ignored family gossip. With a very recent brutal murder to discuss, he felt that the Crowe kin would have considered that more than enough to keep them occupied rather than concerning themselves about whether or not he and Imogen were 'living in sin'.

The cart jogged down the narrow lane which was ablaze with scarlet-blossomed fuchia. Over thick hedges, glimpses of handkerchief fields, a pattern of golden hayricks and black Kerry cows grazing. 'Where are we going?' asked Faro.

Turning to him, Imogen smiled. 'Up yonder, beyond the cliff path, there's a wood with a waterfall that drifts down into the sea. I used to go there often when I was a child. I thought you might like it.'

A few moments later, having safely negotiated a perilously narrow cliff path and with the horse and cart settled by a tree, they climbed towards the hill's summit to be rewarded with a breathtaking panorama. Kerry's long fingers of land extended out across the peninsula. Below them, the shining waters of Lough Beigh stretched right out to Dingle Bay and, beyond, were the first fierce whispers of the Atlantic Ocean.

'Lovely, isn't it?' said Imogen and, pouring him a glass of wine, she told him about Peg and Will who had been laid to rest two days ago and how the wedding feast had become their funeral wake. Still deeply shocked, she found it difficult to describe the murder and, keeping it as brief as possible, with a convulsive shudder, she shook her head. 'Uncle Desmond will give you all the details. He's hoping that you will help him make an arrest.'

'An arrest?'

'Sure. The local police—well, it's beyond the local Garda. Young Conn has never had more than a bit of poaching to deal with.'

'Wait a bit—who is this Uncle Desmond?'

She stared at him. 'Sure now, I've told you about him before. He's more of a cousin really but he was that bit older and it seemed more respectful to call him Uncle when I was a child. He's one of your lot—a detective in Dublin.' Pausing, she looked at him for a response. 'Don't you remember, when we first met, that was just about the only thing we had in common?' she persisted.

Faro nodded. He had a vague recollection of that boasted law connection but, at the time, there had been more urgent and pressing matters to engage his attention than such a coincidence prompted by the abrasive woman writer. He could smile now at the memory of that first meeting. Little had either of them foreseen what lay ahead and how, one day, anger and resentment might undergo such a dramatic change.

'Uncle Desmond's retired now,' Imogen went on. 'He came home to Carasheen a few months ago. After the murder, he got straight in touch with Dublin and they promised to send reinforcements but, meanwhile, asked if he would take over the case and arrest the killers.'

'So they knew who they were?' queried Faro.

'Oh, yes—all three of them,' she said grimly. 'This will be the easiest case either of you has ever tackled. You see, there was a witness—Paddy, a sweet lad, but tuppence short of a shilling, as we say over here. Bit of a peeping Tom too, likes to follow lovers, watch them—that sort of thing. Annoys some folk but there's no real harm in him.' A particularly nasty habit though, thought Faro, staring uncomfortably over his shoulder at the rows of apparently innocent bushes and trees.

'Paddy saw the murder and the Donnellys' killers—the three Cara brothers, the unholy trinity, as folk call them. They live in the big house but no servants will stay there and the best they can get is gypsy children.' She shuddered. 'According to the few who have ever been in Cara House—they inherited it two years ago—they live in complete squalor.

Their father, Sir Michael Cara and the generations before him have been Carasheen's feudal lords, our landowners, right back to the time when tyranny was imposed on Ireland by Elizabeth of England. As you will realise from that, they are Anglo-Irish in origin, regarding themselves as more fiercely Irish than the Celtic peasantry but staying loyal to the hated English crown, fighting their battles on land and sea and sending their sons to be educated at English universities. Sir Michael did well enough by Carasheen but not by his sons. Their mother died young and folk said he never got over that and let the three boys run wild. After his second wife, who was English, also died in what many considered mysterious circumstances, he seemed to give up, go to pieces and let the estate go to rack and ruin.'

Pausing, she smiled wryly. 'That pedigree herd of Kerry cows—you've seen some of them in the fields we passed as we came up the road—breeding them was once his pride and joy.'

'How did he die?' Faro asked.

'Poor man, folk said he took to the bottle, had a stroke, fell down the stairs at Cara House and broke his neck. After that, his sons decided to turn the clock back to the feudal system.' She shrugged. 'They have been terrorising the village ever since.'

'What sort of terrorising?'

'Everything from droit de seigneur to

11

blackmail—protection money from the richer farmers. If they don't pay up, then bad things happen to their cattle, beatings, barns burnt, animals slaughtered, horses stolen and so forth. As for the inn and the village shop, they reckon both are there to keep them supplied with whiskey and groceries without any payment being made.'

A very unpleasant picture of life in Carasheen was emerging for Faro as he said, 'And this lad Paddy actually saw them kill the young couple.'

'Oh, yes, and he brought back the axe as evidence.'

Faro's mind was racing ahead. 'People don't usually murder without reason, Imogen. And an axe seems an odd choice of weapon . . .'

'Peg and Will were taking the short cut through the wood where the Cara boys were chopping down trees. No peat fires for them— they use the trees for firewood.'

'Motive?' asked Faro.

Imogen shook her head. 'They don't need any motive for violence. Anyone whose shadow crosses their path, who looks sideways at them, is enough. You have to understand,' she added desperately, 'these aren't normal naughty boys we are dealing with. These three are monsters—wicked mad monsters . . .'

'Proven murder is still punishable by death,' Faro said grimly. 'And wicked mad monsters can't be allowed to get away with it. Surely that

12

is why your Uncle Desmond has been put in charge? I expect Dublin will want them arrested and brought to trial.'

'Sure—and this will be the easiest case either of you have ever handled.'

'Wait a moment, you said that before. I thought it was a slip of the tongue.'

She looked away from him, gazed towards the sparkling horizon. He demanded, 'Precisely what has this to do with me, Imogen?'

A smile. 'He wants you to give him a hand. Help him make the arrest.'

'He wants what?'

'He hopes you might take over the case,' Imogen said weakly.

2

Faro was appalled. The very last thing he wanted was to be involved in another murder case. In someone else's country was bad enough but to be brought in quite unofficially and quite unwillingly at the stage when the bodies and all the evidence had been buried days before he arrived made it even worse.

'I cannot possibly do this. What about the local policeman?'

But Imogen cut short his protests, saying hastily, 'You must help, Faro. Our policeman

13

Conn O'Flynn went to the door to question them—a brave lad, doing what he sees as his duty, but hopelessly inexperienced in serious crimes, utterly helpless against them. Imagine the scene. They wanted to know what was this nonsense about them killing the Donnellys. Where was his proof? A witness? That village idiot. Who would believe him? They threw him out bodily, kicked him down the steps. Threatened him with worse if he ever darkened their doors again.'

Pausing for a moment to let this sink in, she said desperately, 'Don't you see how helpless we all are, Faro? Only you and Uncle Desmond are experienced detectives capable of dealing with such a situation. No one here in Carasheen has the authority or the experience.'

How about those reinforcements Dublin promised, he was about to say when she turned to him imploringly. 'There is another problem if you don't see it. Uncle Desmond in his retirement is now one of our community here. And, like everyone else, his existence—his personal safety—depends on steering well away from the Cara boys. He has a very nice home, peace and quiet and he wants it to stay that way. If he crossed them, well . . .' Her sigh and the grim shake of her head allowed him to complete the picture.

What about my retirement and our lives together, thought Faro, with rising feelings of indignation as she continued in a somewhat mollifying tone:

'He thought that you, being a stranger and a famous detective, might wield more power.'

Faro ignored that and asked, 'Does anyone know what the Cara lads had against the Donnellys?'

Imogen shrugged. 'The rumour was that Peg was delivering eggs to the house—she keeps hens. They were drunk and they raped her. It's a very sordid story but these things happen here. Will was away in Tralee at the time and she swore they got her pregnant.'

Faro took this in. Logically, the murder should have been by the outraged Will defending his sweetheart's virtue rather than the other way round.

'What happened to the baby?'

'Peg miscarried.' Something in Imogen's tone hinted that this particular miscarriage had been assisted and debarred further questioning.

She regarded him sadly as she unwrapped the sandwiches. 'You must help, Faro. When you meet the Caras, you'll see what it's like. You'll get the same reply as Conn. They will laugh and say, "We know nothing about a murder. Prove it." And, if Paddy is pushed forward, if he dares, they'll just laugh and say again, "Who is going to take the word of the village simpleton against us? If any do, then they had been better watch out, for we have long memories and their lives won't be worth living." '

Faro's appetite for Imogen's delicious picnic had faded away. Why had he ever come to Kerry? Why hadn't he arranged to meet her in Paris or in Heidelberg where they had many friends? Anywhere but here!

At that moment, as he watched a train steaming across the country in the direction of Dublin, he wished with all his heart that they were both on it and heading away from the last thing he ever wanted—yet another murder case.

*   *   *

The sky clouded over. A sudden chill in the air faded the bright colours and turned the landscape into a washed-out watercolour. Trees and bushes shed vivid greens as the cool breeze echoed like a melancholy dirge, turning their leaves inside out.

'I'm afraid we're in for a shower,' said Imogen.

Faro's depression deepened as he watched her scoop up the sandwiches and hastily repack the hamper.

He eyed it regretfully—so much for the picnic. Hardly time for half a glass of wine. The horror of the young wedding guests' brutal murder had destroyed all thoughts of what he had expected and so eagerly anticipated as his introduction to Carasheen and a happy reunion with Imogen.

The brooding sky released its first raindrops and Faro took the warning to heart, guessing that, when it rained in this part of Ireland, it was seldom a mere shower but would last, heavy and unrelenting, for some time.

As they clambered downhill and boarded the gig, Imogen took the reins and the horse trotted down the narrow lane. From under the large umbrella he held aloft, Faro glimpsed a group of houses, a rural nest succoured by sheltering green hills and pastureland. Many of the houses crouched under thatching and a church steeple bravely pierced the glowering sky. Even distantly, it presented a picturesque scene where a stranger might wish to linger.

'Carasheen?' he said.

Imogen nodded and pointed to the right. 'That's Cara House.'

On the hill above the village, a tall square grey house stared down upon them over the trees and Faro guessed that the whole village must be observable from its upper windows. An excellent vantage point for anyone with a telescope making it their business to keep a firm eye on comings and goings.

As the lane widened into a road surrounding a common with an ancient Celtic cross, Imogen pointed towards the far side. 'There's the Cara Arms. But perhaps you'd rather see Uncle Desmond first. I'll take you

17

there.'

Faro smiled. Her anxious tone and nervous glance in his direction hinted that perhaps the detective from Dublin had been waiting for him somewhat urgently and that she had promised this visit.

'Just let me leave my luggage at the inn,' said Faro, 'and then we'll go and see him.'

*　　　*　　　*

But there was no need of that. Desmond Crowe was expecting them. Seated by the inn's window overlooking the green, he had been there for some considerable time consulting his watch with increasing anxiety ever since Imogen had gone off to the station to meet Faro's train.

His patience was running out. Waiting made it seem like hours had gone by and it was with a great sigh of relief that he recognised the trotting pony cart, Imogen's red hair and the man folding an umbrella at her side. Desmond smiled—they were a handsome couple indeed. He was proud of his young cousin Imogen.

The rain had momentarily ceased and the tall man helping her alight was unmistakably Faro. He had done some research on the Inspector from Edinburgh City Police who had also served as a personal detective to Queen Victoria and had saved her life on several occasions during his career.

18

Although Faro was frequently regarded as a Lowland Scot, he was, in fact, an Orcadian and, as they crossed the green towards the inn, Desmond decided that the Viking strain was still evident. Under thick once-fair hair now tarnished with grey, the high cheek-boned face gave no concession to gentle contours but closer inspection revealed stern lines softened by a well-shaped mouth that would have done credit to a Roman sculpture. His full lips hinted at gentleness and humour too. Were they also an indication of vulnerability?

With such a give-away, many a wiser man would have taken advantage of disguise afforded by the current fashion for facial hair, Desmond thought, stroking his own luxurious beard as he hurried to the door to greet them.

As Imogen made the introductions, Faro's handshake was strong and firm, the eyes shrewd, piercingly blue and slightly narrowed —as might have become a watchful Viking invader. Desmond repressed an inward chuckle. Put a horned helmet on this man and you'd have the ultimate Viking—a quite extraordinary resemblance.

He smiled. 'Well, well, so this is the famous Chief Inspector Faro.'

'Not any more,' was Faro's modest reply.

Desmond smiled. 'Come now, only the very famous are invited to address learned philosophical societies in Ireland.'

Faro gave him a quick glance. Was there a

19

hint of envy there? he wondered, following Desmond into the snug where a substantial dram of whiskey was immediately slid across the table towards him.

'Slainte!' A very welcome toast. Faro relaxed and so did Imogen, who gazed delightedly from one to the other.

Casually taking stock of Desmond, Faro sensed that he was also nervous about this first encounter. A tall man, about his own age, entirely bald, his hair having slid down into sideburns, moustache and beard, all of which hid the lower part of his face. All that was visible now were his bespectacled eyes. Large dark eyes full of melancholy, with an uneasy life of their own. Restless, they darted about the room, assessing every shadow, exploring every corner, never settling on either Imogen or himself as they spoke.

Faro was used to making quick assessments and first glances told him more about most people than they ever guessed. Here was a perturbed and very worried man. Those haunted eyes, mirrors of the soul, were very revealing to an observer of Faro's calibre. Clearly Desmond Crowe had not found happiness or contentment in his retirement. Was he married or a widower? Faro had not had time to find that out from Imogen. But it seemed that whatever he had searched for and hoped to recapture in Carasheen had eluded him.

'So you are at the inn here,' he was saying. 'I would have invited you to stay at my cottage— I feel badly about that. You see, I have only one spare room, at present occupied by an American visitor here to research his family roots . . .' Desmond stopped suddenly and Faro intercepted a quick warning glance from Imogen as he continued hastily, 'There's a maid's room in the attic if you're not entirely happy. I could move her out but I couldn't recommend it.'

'I absolutely forbid you to do that, sir,' said Faro. 'I would not think of causing such inconvenience.' The dark, grim, panelled snug, with its spittoons and decades of stale tobacco smoke seeping through the walls, hinted gravely that the rooms upstairs might not be a great improvement but he managed a hopeful and reassuring, 'I'm sure I will be quite comfortable here.'

Desmond brightened at that. It brought forth an eager recommendation about Tom's good food and wine, excellent beds—and the warning that he was a bit of a gossip.

'He'll have your whole life story in the first ten minutes and the whole of Carasheen will know all there is to be known about you, including some of his own embellishments and speculations, of course, in half an hour.'

Faro smiled and Imogen chuckled. 'Not this gentleman, Uncle. He could give clams lessons in closeness.'

'Good at keeping secrets, are you?' laughed Desmond, hastily topping up his emptied glass. 'A necessity in our profession, of course.'

Suddenly his face darkened. He nodded towards Imogen: 'You have told him?'

Imogen sighed. 'Yes, Uncle. But I left most of the details . . . to you. I couldn't somehow . . . bring myself . . .' She fell silent with a weary shake of her head.

Desmond regarded her with compassion and put a hand on her arm. 'I don't suppose you want to hear it all again. Well, later will do.'

Imogen stood up. 'No, please get on with it, Uncle. Time is getting short. It doesn't get any easier to bear. The sooner you get it settled the better for everyone—except Peg and Will.' With her eyes filling with sudden tears, she turned to Faro, 'I'll come back for you. Maeve will have made a meal for us.'

She looked across at Desmond who nodded and said: 'Give us half an hour.'

Imogen, relieved, smiled at Faro. 'See you later, then.'

They stood up politely and watched her leave. Faro thought he had never heard her so cold and impersonal. A polite stranger.

3

Still reading some unspoken and unhappy message into Imogen's departure, Faro heard Desmond singing her praises. 'A fine lass, indeed. The whole family are proud of her. And no wonder. All that she has been through —for Ireland.' Another sigh and then, suddenly businesslike, the detective in the interviewing room took over from the genial host. Sitting opposite Faro, leaning his elbows on the table and regarding him shrewdly, he said, 'A dreadful business. Both those fine bairns killed, slaughtered like sheep. Paddy— has she told you about Paddy?' Faro nodded and Desmond continued, 'Sure, Paddy saw it all. They got the lad first—seized him from behind—the girl screamed, went to drag them off him . . . You can guess the rest—both were felled by that axe. God knows they died immediately but it was a terrible scene.' For a moment, those restless eyes were still—wide open with the picture of horror he had seen indelibly seared on to them.

He shuddered and went on, 'No one would believe Paddy when he came back. He doesn't speak very well—his tongue is too big for his mouth and he stutters. They could only gather that Peg and Will had crossed the path of the Caras while they were chopping wood. But when he showed them the axe they—every one of them—ran after him to where Peg and Will were lying dead and bloodied, in their Sunday best clothes.'

Pausing, he put his hands over his face. 'Awful it was, awful. They came for the doctor but it was too late for that. Then they came for me, knowing the police lad Conn couldn't cope. And I have to tell you, Mr Faro, that, although I have witnessed terrible scenes, this was one I'll remember until my dying day. I sent a telegraph to Dublin immediately, saying that we would need help and this was beyond a local village policeman. Conn goes all to pieces if he comes face to face with a poacher. Dublin said they would send someone down with a back-up team but meanwhile asked if I would take over—organise the inquest and so forth.' Pausing again, he smiled sadly at Faro. 'It is a huge responsibility they have set me and, quite frankly, I am not sure that I am up to it any more. Certainly not single-handed,' he added pathetically. 'So I will be greatly obliged, sir, if you would give me your assistance.'

Although he no longer had Imogen's eye upon him, Faro knew he could not refuse. The old urge was still there, to see justice done, whether he wanted it or not, whether it was inconvenient or not. He could not turn his back, gather up Imogen and walk away from the brutal murder of two innocent victims. So he said, 'I'll do what I can. Are we to arrest the

Cara lads on Paddy's evidence?'

Desmond nodded. 'That's the general idea but we must walk warily. Conn took the axe into custody, for what it's worth.' He shrugged uncomfortably. 'Those young villains are not going to like it and others—the folk of Carasheen—might be made to suffer. No one has ever questioned them yet and they believe they are above the law. So arrogant, Mr Faro, riding about on their three black horses as if they own the entire universe. Folk speak of them as that unholy trinity. Even their names. Matthew—Mat—he's the heir, then there's Mark, then Luke. There was a fourth, the youngest, John, if God or the Devil had willed it to complete this quartet of villainy. But John mercifully departed this life with his poor mother.' Desmond shook his head. 'Villains with Biblical names, the four apostles. We've often wondered what John would have been like had he survived.'

Faro was no coward—he had faced terrible odds in his long career. A picture was taking shape in his mind. Two detectives retired and no longer young, well past their best days of fitness, plus the village policeman, whom he had yet to meet, who, by all accounts, was young, highly nervous and inexperienced. Three of them riding up that hill, confidently striding up to that grey-faced mansion, hammering on the front door, sternly accusing the Cara brothers of murder and arresting these three active strong vicious youths who were so keen on brutality and violence. Then bringing them down to Carasheen in handcuffs, keeping them under lock and key in a house near the common, one of those fragile-looking thatched dwellings, Faro supposed, that went by the imposing and unbelievable designation of 'local police station'. His imaginary journey continued with them leading the three villains to docilely board the train in a jail van, helpfully provided by the Dublin police, in which to carry them to the High Courts for trial. He almost laughed out loud. If it had not been so serious, the whole idea would be ludicrous.

Desmond coughed nervously as he solemnly watched Faro's reactions. 'As with all unpleasant tasks, sir, the sooner we get it over, the better. I think, in the best interests of everyone concerned, we should proceed as soon as possible, confront the unholy trinity and see what happens.'

Faro regarded him desperately. Had the man no imagination? What he was suggesting wasn't merely unpleasant—it was absolute madness. Trying to sound calm, he managed to gasp, 'I think we should hold out until those reinforcements arrive.'

Desmond shook his head. 'Better not, Mr Faro. Can you imagine what would happen in this village if the Cara boys got wind of that? What a vengeance they would take?' While

Faro was considering a suitable argument, taking his silence as acceptance, Desmond gave an audible sigh and, pausing to rub his beard, he regarded Faro thoughtfully. 'I thought you would be particularly good at confrontation, sir, with all your vast experience. No doubt you can put the fear of death into them,' he added heartily and, before Faro could utter a word of protest, added, 'you being a stranger here and a famous detective.'

Faro shook his head. 'A very forlorn hope, I fear, from all I have heard of these villains so far,' he said as he visualised Desmond's suggestion of a confrontation as it would be seen through the mocking, derisive eyes of the three Cara boys. They would scoff at the idea of two old men and a scared boy coming to arrest them. As for the ex-detective's hopes that Faro's presence would scare them, that they had ever heard of him or his reputation was not only unlikely but, in less grim circumstances, would have seemed not only preposterous but completely naive and even laughable.

'Tomorrow, then, shall we say?' asked Desmond, mightily pleased and relieved. With the time arranged, he left feeling that it had not been such a struggle to enlist Faro's help as he had originally imagined. A most agreeable man.

*   *   *

After seeing him off the premises, Faro found a silent shadow hovering to show him upstairs to his room. A great shambling bear of a man was Tom Kelly, the curious resemblance borne out by a forehead so narrow as to appear like a mere naked track separating fierce grey eyebrows from the matching bush of unruly grey hair.

Faro followed him up the dark brown staircase with its cracking paint and abominably creaking boards. At the top, a door was opened to reveal a shabby room of monastic severity. It was furnished, if such a word implying luxury and comfort could be stretched to apply to the scene before him, with bed, chair and washstand table. There was one small window and Faro marched across to it hopefully. This was not the lovely heart-warming landscape he had been looking forward to, with perhaps a glimpse of the Atlantic Ocean. Instead, it stared bleakly across a narrow alley on to a blank wall. Sounds of activity, the clash of pans, wafts of steam and smells of bygone meals, which floated upwards, suggested that the room was situated directly above the kitchen.

Sternly he regarded the single bed and the crucifix nailed to the wall above it. He suspected that the mattress was hard and unyielding and, although the sheets were white and clean, he was also to discover that the pillows were so robustly feathered they resembled stone boulders gathered from the shore. He made no comment. Perhaps Tom was disappointed in this reception of his accommodation for, with a defiant stare, he said, 'I'll leave you with it. Breakfast at eight.'

Faro gazed despairingly round the room which defied any prospect of the romantic dalliance with Imogen that he yearned for. Impatiently throwing down his luggage, he said aloud, 'So much for dreams.'

How he had looked forward to seeing Kerry but now, before his visit had properly begun, it had turned sour on him—not only sour but dangerous. He did not care to think too much about what he had taken on as an obligement to Imogen's Uncle Des. The Cara boys boasted that they could make life not worth living. In the case of two retired detectives well past their best days, this might even imply the death of both of them.

Impatiently awaiting Imogen's arrival gave Faro plenty of time to consider what he was letting himself in for. He knew the importance of proceeding with great caution at the beginning of a case. He was aware that he should be in full possession of all the facts, including having an accurate timetable of the incidents as they had occurred. He set great store by having a close examination of the scene of crime and interviewing any witnesses

29

where such existed. But none of this was going to be possible before he accompanied Desmond Crowe and plunged headlong into a disastrous and perhaps even fatal confrontation with that unholy trinity, the Cara boys. He sighed. In this case, the evidence and other matters of vital importance were without a satisfactory explanation. They had only the word of the simple Paddy, who claimed to have witnessed the murder, but what was the motive for the Caras' attack on the young couple? All of Faro's previous experience indicated that murder must have a motive but, in this case, no one seemed able to provide one.

He also knew the vital importance of finding out if their behaviour at the wedding had been odd or provocative in any way. A mild-mannered, inoffensive couple by all accounts, what was their house like? Would it yield any interesting clues?

As he sat at the table making notes, the action took him back to his Edinburgh investigations. How he had thought such matters were over forever when he took young Prince George back to Luxoria last year—a fraught and heart-breaking adventure at Her Majesty's wish (or command), leaving him with a secret he must carry untold into eternity. He had emerged fortunate to be alive for such he knew had not been the grim intention of that particular mission. But it had convinced him that this was to be his last venture into crime and mayhem.

Afterwards, he had relaxed and was prepared to enjoy his retirement with the much-travelled Imogen. Now they would go together to all those cities he had read about and dreamed of visiting during his long service with the Edinburgh City Police. With a gesture of disgust, he threw down his pen. What had happened instead to all those plans? An innocent occasion like a family wedding had plunged him into yet another chilling murder case. His thoughts were interrupted by a tap on the door. A maid stood there. 'Miss Crowe to see you, sir.'

'Send her up, please.'

The young maid stared at him, her shocked expression hinting at some improper suggestion. She shook her head. 'Sure now, sir, that ain't allowed. Ladies . . .'—she placed an emphasis on the word as she repeated it— 'ladies are not allowed in gentlemen guests' bedrooms. Ye'll have to come down and see her yerself,' she added virtuously.

Imogen was waiting for him downstairs. Kissing her in full sight of Tom and the customers at the bar, he demanded angrily, 'Did you know about these absurd rules?'

She frowned and, staring defiantly in Tom's direction, he explained about the maid's visit.

Imogen laughed. 'Nonsense, isn't it? But what can we do about it, Faro?'

'Makes us sound like wicked schoolchildren

31

or frustrated lovers.'

She looked at him candidly. 'And are we not just that?' Before he could reply she linked his arm. 'Sure now, don't take on so, Faro. We can meet in my room.'

And at his eager glance she laughed. 'No, you can't stay the night since I share it with Cousin Maeve.' And, when he scowled, she added, 'Sure now, she's very understanding about giving us time together.'

Maeve, she told him, was the mother of the bride who, at present, was honeymooning in the Scottish Highlands with her sea captain husband, blissfully unaware of the dreadful fate that had befallen two of their wedding guests. Maeve's cottage was pretty with a thatched roof. Very old, very comfortable, with a huge kitchen and a peat fire, it warmed his heart and, carrying him back to those long lost childhood days in Orkney, it almost entirely banished his black mood. A huge fish pie, topped with buttered potatoes and cabbage from the garden, followed by a suet pudding did the rest and his well-filled stomach soon had him better disposed towards life in general. Home-brewed ale added to Faro's sense of well being especially as, perhaps warned by Imogen, Maeve refrained from any mention of the recent murders.

Maeve reminded him in looks and bearing of dear old Mrs Brook, erstwhile housekeeper of his home in Edinburgh's Sheridan Place.

She was maybe not quite as much the soul of tact as that lady, however, since Maeve was clearly dying to know if he and Imogen were getting married sometime soon. But he could afford to take smilingly such veiled hints heading his way.

Puzzled that Imogen called him by his surname, she said, 'It doesn't sound quite proper for an . . .' a small hesitation then a bold step forward 'an engaged couple not to be on first name terms.'

Faro laughed. 'Some folk across the water often still call each other Mr and Mrs after many years of marriage.' Then, with a smile, he added, 'I'm called Jeremy.' A bow towards Imogen indicated that she provide the explanation.

Imogen shook her head. 'I thought Jeremy made him sound like a little boy. It didn't seem quite strong and dignified enough for a formidable Chief Inspector of Police when we first met. I got into the habit of calling him Faro then and now I can't change.'

'Jeremy is a nice name. I like it,' said Maeve defiantly.

'Then you call me that,' said Faro.

'And so I shall,' was the reply as Maeve darted a reproachful look in Imogen's direction. Then, with a sigh and laying aside her sewing, she announced, 'I have a few things to do upstairs, then I am for bed, Imogen darling, so you and your young man . . .'

Something must be wrong with her eyesight, Faro decided, as, without batting an eyelid, she continued, 'can enjoy a bit of peace and quiet. I dare say you have lots to talk over. So goodnight, Imogen, and goodnight, Jeremy. Just make yourselves at home.' And, with an arch look that spoke volumes, she left them.

It was good to sit on the old sofa with Imogen's head resting on his shoulder as she asked, 'Comfortable, Faro?'

He smiled and kissed her. 'Not much of a substitute for a fleecy white pillow though, is it?'

Imogen sighed. 'Not a bit as I hoped or planned, I can tell you. Believe me, had there been any way of stopping you coming here, I would have let you know. Uncle Des could have managed somehow—especially once the Dublin folk get around to sending some regular police to help as he asked.'

Faro smiled wryly. He had grave doubts about that promised help arriving in time. 'The die is cast, as the saying goes, and the sooner we get it over with the sooner we two will be able to head back to Dublin and you can do the rest of your research there.'

'I need to be here for a while. Daniel O'Connell was a Kerry man remember.' The clock struck ten and she sighed. 'You had better go, darling. I don't want to keep Maeve awake. She's a light sleeper. You know how it is in the country. Up at dawn to milk the cow and feed the hens—and, in her case, a creche of wee bairns, bright eyed and bushy tailed at five, demanding food and attention.'

Tiptoeing hand in hand to the door, they had a final embrace and she whispered, 'Uncle Des will take you to . . . to where it happened . . . and to meet Paddy. You will need an interpreter to talk to him as he doesn't have the English.'

'What about the young couple's house?'

Imogen shivered. 'Empty, I imagine. Just as they left it. No one will want to live there for a very long time, I fear.' And, placing a hand against his cheek, she added, 'Dearest Faro, I know how awful this is for you. And I can't help blaming myself . . .'

'Nonsense, my dear. All in a day's work,' said Faro with a cheerful confidence he was far from feeling.

Imogen shook her head. 'That isn't true—not now, anyway. And I got you into all this . . .'

Faro placed a hand over her lips and then he kissed her once more. 'You know I cannot refuse. Besides, I never could resist a challenge.' And what a challenge, he thought, as with a sinking heart he walked back to the inn where Tom stared at him from the public bar, his brusque goodnight making sure that his guest was climbing the creaking stair alone.

Surprisingly, he slept well, his dreams free of the nightmare that awaited him—the nightmare that was Carasheen's reality.

35

4

The young maid brought warm water for his ablutions and, as was appropriate considering her anxiety about his moral conduct, swiftly departed with a scared look in his direction. As he shaved, the smell drifting upwards hinted at fried bacon with the possibility of accompanying sausage and eggs. With his appetite aroused, he was greeted unsmilingly but with reasonable politeness by Tom and breakfast was all that he had hoped for. He was downing his second cup of rich, strong, dark tea when the door opened to admit Desmond Crowe, obviously eager to start the day's activities. Taking a seat opposite, he declined tea and toast, saying, 'Just the two of us—it is Conn's day off. He's gone to visit his mother.' And, leaning across the table, he whispered, 'The axe—the evidence, you know, is kept locked in his safe, should you want to see it.'

With no excuse to linger, they emerged from the inn. Outside, the sun was shining brightly but somehow Desmond's remarks about how lucky they were that it was such a fine day fell flat for Faro considering what lay ahead of them.

'I presume you ride a horse,' Desmond said.

'Not very well or very often,' Faro admitted.

'It wasn't a necessary qualification in my Edinburgh days.'

Desmond laughed. 'I guessed that somehow. Everyone rides here but I have other means of travel,' he added, pointing to the inevitable pony cart which was the alternative.

As they drove through the village, Desmond indicated the church and the hall next door where the wedding reception had taken place. They skirted the village and came to a halt at a stile at the end of a tree-lined lane. 'We go on by foot,' said Desmond. 'Along that path is where it happened.'

Faro followed but with little hope of finding any remaining evidence. There were piles of sawn logs and a fallen trunk used as a chopping block but no signs of a struggle— nothing left to suggest that murder had ever taken place. Recent rains had washed away any bloodstains and nature had taken over, healing any scars made by brutal human activity. Underfoot the grass had grown strong and straight again. Faro looked around hopefully. Perhaps he might spot a broken branch or two. As the birds twittered and sang above their heads, he had a sudden vivid mental picture of how that song had once been stilled by the terrible cries coming from beneath those branches. At his side, Desmond said, 'There's nothing here now, is there?' Faro nodded. That there might have been some clues remaining was too much to hope for. It was impossible, even now, to imagine much less describe that terrible murder scene.

'If there had been no witness it would have been unbelievable,' said Desmond solemnly, reminding Faro that the next stage was the visit to Paddy.

'Does he live nearby?'

'No, in Carasheen with the priest, Father McNee. Paddy makes himself useful in the house. Like many who are simple minded, he is exceptionally strong. He helps in the church. The father was sorry for him when his mother died. She was a decent woman, deeply religious and so, we gather from Father McNee, is her son. He knows the Bible at least.'

Desmond sighed. 'The father is one of the few people who understands Paddy's speech. It needs patience even for those of us who have the Irish.'

A few minutes later, they were at the church. As Desmond thrust open the door, Faro momentarily found the mingled smells of wax candles and incense overpowering. The priest, who came forward to greet them, had hardly any more flesh on his bones than the skeletal figures of mortality decorating the monuments on the walls. The bones of his skull were evident for there was not a hair on his head or on his face and the colour of his deep-set eyes was lost behind heavy eyelids.

His voice too was thin, reedy, hardly above a whisper.

Faro was surprised. As he waited for Desmond to introduce him, he realised he had expected a village priest to look like Friar Tuck or like those depicted in Shakespeare's plays, round, well-fed and merry. Desmond was explaining the necessity for this interview with Paddy. The priest's eyes swivelled constantly in Faro's direction, plainly ill at ease with the suggestion and regarding this stranger to Carasheen with a mixture of distaste and suspicion.

'I don't want you upsetting poor Paddy. I absolutely forbid it,' he said sternly to Desmond, whom he guessed might have the greater authority. Then, turning to Faro, 'It was a terrible thing for the poor lad to have to witness. You can take my word for what happened. I had the whole story from him and he never lies.' He paused, waiting for some comment or assent from Faro. There was none. With a despairing sigh, he went on, 'A terrible sight for the village when he ran back to the hall, brandishing . . .' He closed his eyes against that vision. 'The axe. And screaming— screaming words that none of us understood.' Again he paused. 'When we got him calmed down, that was terrible too.' He frowned and bit his lip. 'There are those who are unsure about Paddy,' he added candidly. 'Perhaps some imagined he had finally lost what wits he ever had and had gone mad.'

Picturing the scene, Faro found that not too difficult to understand as the priest continued. 'Fortunately, I was able to reassure them, convince them that they were in no mortal danger from Paddy. I could guarantee that he has never lied to me. He told me the whole story—what he had seen—again in the confessional.' And turning sharply to Faro, who he thought might be sceptical, he added, 'The lad is deeply religious. And he is certainly innocent. If I need further proof, everyone knew he was exceedingly fond of Peg and Will Donnelly and they thought the world of him. Although they teased him, scolded him about spying on them, they treated him tolerantly, as one would a lively, exuberant puppy.'

'What can you tell Inspector Faro about Peg and Will?' Desmond interrupted.

'They were good Catholics, a fine young couple who came to Mass regularly and to confession.' It wasn't much to go on but Faro knew better than to ask what he most wanted to know—whether they had ever indicated in the confessional anything that might be of importance, anything that might be a clue to their murder, particularly about the lad Paddy.

'It would be very helpful if we could have a word with Paddy,' said Faro.

'Desmond has already talked to him several times.'

'I did so immediately—Inspector Faro

40

knows that—but he will need you to interpret
. . .' They were interrupted by a sound like an
animal in pain and, as they turned round,
there was Paddy standing in the door of the
church, watching them and, no doubt, listening
too—if he understood a word they were
saying. Speaking to him in Gaelic, Father
McNee invited him to come in. Paddy came
down the aisle twisting his bonnet in his hands.
Staring at Faro, he walked round him as if he
was some new species of creature he had never
before encountered. At that moment, Faro
was considering wryly the cruelty of nature.
The young man—who could have been any
age from eighteen to forty—had once almost
had the beauty of the angels who adorned the
church walls. Blonde curls, wide-set blue eyes
and classical features that should have added
up to the handsomest of men. There was only
one difference—his eyes were a mere fraction
out of alignment, as were his chin and mouth.
He looked like some out of focus picture of a
fallen angel painted by a busy artist who was
irritated and impatient with his subject.

Faro realised by Paddy's sudden change of
expression that Desmond and the priest were
now discussing the murder again with him.
The result was terrible. He placed his hands
over his ears to try to block his terror. Sobs
racked him, he flung the bonnet on the floor
and stamped his foot on it, as if it was some
creature that had done him an injury. He

41

roared, in a great voice, some words repeated over and over in Irish and lost on Faro.

The priest put a thin arm about his shoulders, patting him, murmuring soothing words as one would to a fractious child. It had the required effect. Paddy stared at them, his huge eyes welling with tears. Father McNee picked up the bonnet, handed it to him and, shaking his head, indicated to Desmond and Faro that they should leave now. The interview, if it could be so called, with the one witness was at an end.

Leading them to the church door, he whispered, 'Come back later, when I have had time to explain it all and calm him down.' Once out of the church and into the morning sunshine, Faro realised that this was the nearest he would ever come to questioning Paddy. He would have to take Desmond's word for it—and the priest's—that the lad was totally honest and he wasn't looking at the killer of Peg and Will, which he had to admit, in all truth, he had been seriously considering. It was, after all, a logical conclusion. Perhaps all that good-natured teasing, which the people of the village thought so little of, had humiliated him, thrown him over the edge.

Faro sighed. So little was known about such aspects of human behaviour but, from many years of experience, Faro was perfectly aware that the first to discover the body and report the crime, whether bringing the murder weapon or not, was very often proved to be the killer. But, apparently, not this time. Still, it seemed a regrettable omission not to interview Paddy in the manner instilled in him over many years as a detective and regarded as normal procedure for a main witness.

Faro shook his head. The thought of sitting with an interpreter, the stern and disapproving Father McNee, and questioning that poor creature, inflicting further cruelty on that tortured mind, was beyond him. This was just one more frustration in a murder case forced upon him, an investigation outwith any previous experience that had ever come his way in Edinburgh.

Desmond was waiting for him to make some comment. 'I shall have to take your word and Father McNee's for it,' he said. 'You both seem absolutely certain that Paddy is innocent and that he did not run amok with an axe.'

Desmond gave a shocked exclamation. 'That just isn't possible if you knew anything about Paddy.'

'And I'm not likely ever to know that at first hand, am I?' said Faro wearily. 'But I should like to know something more about Peg and Will than the scant information I have had from anyone so far. In particular, I would like to see over their house.'

'I will take you there gladly,' was the accommodating response. 'But I hardly think it will yield any vital clues.'

43

And, as they boarded the pony cart and sped through the summer greenery of narrow lanes, Faro had little hope of that either.

5

As they approached the little croft, Desmond told Faro something of the background of the tragic young couple. 'Peg Foster was an orphan, a foundling put in the care of the church home. Last year, she went to the market at Tralee to sell eggs from the home and Will Donnelly was up from Cork selling his pigs.'

So the lad was a newcomer, thought Faro. That might have some significance.

'Anyway, Will came into some money, bought the croft and they were married.'

Coming into money was perhaps also significant. 'Where did the money come from?' he asked.

Desmond shrugged. 'No one knew but Peg bought a few hens and began selling eggs.'

'That was how she encountered the Caras?'

'Correct—looking for new customers, she went up to the house with her basket. And we know what happened then,' he said grimly.

'Surely she knew something about their reputation.'

Desmond shook his head and sighed. 'I'm

44

afraid neither she nor Will were particularly bright. Simple gentle souls, lost in each other, in their own lives and their own tiny world. They didn't look far beyond that, went to Mass regularly and one can only presume that Peg believed that, being a married woman, she would be safe from the attention of the Cara lads.'

Rape was bad enough but being made pregnant . . . Yet her husband did nothing about that and it ended with them both being murdered. It still didn't make sense to Faro. It simply wasn't logical and, when he said so, Desmond shook his head, 'Since she lost the baby anyway, I expect Will thought it was best to let sleeping dogs lie.'

'Or sleeping villains!' said Faro. 'But Peg's rape could have been the reason for the murder. Did the Cara lads taunt him or, faced with them, did Will's feelings of rage overcome his determination to remain silent? Had Will made the initial move, then the subsequent tragedy would have made sense.'

As Desmond replied, 'According to Paddy the attack was unprovoked', Faro wondered if things were always back to front in Carasheen. The witness report came from a simple-minded lad, thought Faro wryly, a peeping Tom who loved to watch lovers but lived with the priest who swore that Paddy never told a lie and would never imperil his immortal soul. Doubtless all the good Catholics of Carasheen

45

were eager to accept his word as absolute truth. It might well be so but Faro's years of experience demanded more than this insubstantial evidence. He wanted to know where exactly Paddy had been standing at the time and if there was any possibility of taking him back so that he could show them the spot from where he had witnessed the scene. Faro would have been prepared to bet that he had kept well out of sight and was certainly not within earshot of the exact words that might have been exchanged between the Cara brothers and the Donnellys.

As for Will's sudden fortune and the termination of Peg's pregnancy, he wanted to know a lot more about that too. He made a mental note that a talk to the local doctor might be worthwhile. They left the pony cart and walked through a once neat and tidy garden that was already beginning to look unkempt and overgrown. The pigs and hens were apparently being looked after by a neighbour. Desmond pushed open the door and led Faro into the kitchen. Beyond, he could see a parlour and bedroom. In their simple furnishings, the neat and tidy rooms managed to reflect something of their owners' characters. In the parlour, with its handmade rugs on the floor, there were cheap wooden tables and chairs and a holy statue, plus a few religious pictures. And the kitchen's gleaming pots and pans were still pristine enough to have been wedding presents. The bedroom had a bed with a knitted bedspread on it, but no headboard, a cupboard for holding clothes and an ancient well-worn chest of drawers.

Faro looked around. The house certainly did not suggest an abundance of evidence. Everything was fairly basic and impersonal—as if their few months of occupation had not been time enough to leave any imprint, any hallmark of possession. Opening one of the drawers of the chest, his thoughts were confirmed by folded linen, obviously unused wedding presents with cards still attached. There was also a photograph album. Desmond was looking over his shoulder as he skimmed through the contents. 'Mostly postcards gathered from Dear-knows-where,' he said. Postcards were the current fashion. 'Thinking of you in . . .'—a faster smarter way of communicating with family and friends, especially for those who found writing letters tedious or difficult.

'Everyone sends them these days—the lazy way,' Desmond interpreted his thoughts and Faro nodded vaguely, guiltily aware that he now gratefully availed himself of this convenient method of keeping in touch with his own family. Desmond's statement reminded him that he must buy some postcards. It was a sadly long time since he had written to Emily in Orkney or Rose in America—he used his travels in Europe with

Imogen as the grand excuse for such an omission.

Desmond was turning the pages of the album. Among the postcards, there was a wedding photo of the Donnellys and, alongside it, a rather faded sepia and outdated image of a young man. Turning it over there was no name or identification of the subject, only a blurred photographer's name with 'Dublin' legible. 'Parent, do you think?' Faro asked.

Desmond was studying the photo intently. Frowning, he shook his head. 'I can't say. I know nothing of the lass's origins. Maybe someone she met in the home.' Then, with a sigh, he added, 'We'll never know.' Faro left him and continued his search for something in that impeccably neat and impersonal house which might identify the Donnellys with their killers.

Desmond reappeared. 'Shall we go then?'

Still wrestling with the frustration of that complete lack of evidence, Faro stared at him. 'Go? Where had you in mind?'

'Cara House, of course. I thought that was decided.' Desmond sounded braver than he felt.

Faro shook his head. 'Not without an official member of the local constabulary.'

'Conn?' Desmond laughed. 'He won't be back until tomorrow—besides he's useless.'

'Useless or no, he officially represents the

48

law in Carasheen. You are a retired detective and I am merely a visitor here . . .'

'But . . .'

Faro cut short his protest. 'I for one am definitely not moving until Conn returns. We cannot legally make arrests without him or a sight of those Dublin reinforcements you were promised—preferably with both.' Shaking his head, he added sternly, 'At the moment, I want a lot more evidence than I have heard and seen so far.'

'Evidence?' Desmond made it sound like a new word in the vocabulary.

'Yes, I need firm facts rather than circumstantial evidence before I take another step in this matter.'

'I thought I had told you all I know,' was the reproachful reply. 'Is that not enough?'

'You have been most helpful but I need to talk to the doctor.'

'I don't see how Dr Neill can help you.'

Faro smiled patiently. 'If you will forgive me for pointing out that you have newly returned to Carasheen after a long absence and Conn is a mere youth. But am I right in presuming that the doctor has been here for many years?'

'All his life.'

'Exactly. Then the chances are that he can fill in some of the missing background concerning the murdered girl. Perhaps also for the Cara family—he must have written the death certificates for their father, mother and stepmother.'

Desmond gave a weary sigh and Faro did not care to remind him that such practicalities as he was asking for had been routine procedure in his Edinburgh career. Every person who had any connection, however remote, with the murder victim was closely questioned.

Desmond looked glum and said huffily, 'Well now, if we aren't going anywhere, I have other matters to attend to. I'll show you where Dr Neill lives though you'll be lucky to find him at home at this hour of the day,' he added and, as the pony cart approached the common, he pointed across the square to a handsome stone-built Georgian house with a neat garden. A notice in the window declared, 'Surgery. Apply within.'

Parking the pony cart by the gate, Desmond said, 'You must realise there are few calls on the doctor's time—folks here are very healthy—and he spends a lot of time out fishing in his boat down by the harbour.' The door was opened by a woman Desmond addressed as Margaret. She informed them that Dr Neill was at home and he would be pleased to meet Mr Faro who was aware again, as they were ushered into the consulting room, of the careful scrutiny with which he was received in Carasheen. An awesome reputation as a detective, played up no doubt by Imogen's relatives, he decided, accounted for his cautious reception.

For a moment, it looked as though Desmond, cordially invited to take a drink, might stay. Politely he shook his head, 'Mr Faro has some questions for you, Peter. I'll be leaving you to it then.' As the door closed on him, Neill led the way across the hall and Faro was gratified to observe that the interior of the house was as neat as the exterior promised. Everywhere there was the woman's touch, the good smell of furniture polish, flowers in pretty vases, with masculinity sternly reasserting itself in the oak-panelled study with wall-high bookshelves, leather armchairs and a very large desk.

Invited to take a seat, Faro was asked, 'Questions, sir. How can I help you?'

'Mr Crowe has asked my help with the Donnelly murders . . .'

A shocked exclamation of 'Dreadful, dreadful!' came from the doctor who had the prosperous look of authority. He was a well-groomed, well-preserved fifty-year-old, with a well-trimmed fashionable moustache, neat beard and a bedside manner as smooth as the pillows his patients rested their heads upon. Taking the other side of the desk, he placed his fingertips together and leaned forward in an attentive manner—an attitude that reminded Faro fondly of his dear stepson Dr Vince Laurie. Was this, he wondered, the traditional doctor's pose as set out in the

51

textbook for young medical students and guaranteed to inspire confidence in their apprehensive patients?

'I gather you have been resident in Carasheen for some years, Dr Neill.'

'Indeed, yes. Born and bred, sir, born and bred. Did my medical training and qualified in Dublin, then came back home. Margaret and I have never had the slightest desire to live anywhere else, especially with the family so reluctant to leave Kerry.'

Faro thought he made it sound very foreign indeed as, pausing to open an unseen drawer in the desk, he extracted a bottle of whiskey and poured out a generous dram which he set before Faro. 'Your good health, sir.' And, taking a sip, he added, 'Sure now and this was a piece of paradise in the old days when Sir Michael Cara was alive. A great chap, a great chap he was. Not like these young villains he left behind. He must turn in his grave when he sees what Carasheen has become . . .'

They were interrupted as the door opened and Margaret came in with soda bread, oatcakes and cheese. The doctor introduced her to Faro. A still-pretty woman in her fifties with white hair and classical features, she looked strikingly like an older version of Imogen. So he wasn't surprised when Neill said, 'Margaret is a Crowe—I married into the clan.'

While they wrestled with Margaret's

delicious offering, which went so splendidly with the whiskey, there was quite a bit more talk involving confusing relationships in Carasheen. At last, dusting down the crumbs, they set depleted plates back on the tray.

Neill was about to resume the conversation when the grandfather clock interrupted, cutting short any such intentions by the dramatic onset of a stately and somewhat loud and lengthy harmony, concluding with twelve solemn chimes. The doctor immediately drew out his watch, consulted it carefully, clicked it shut and said, 'I have a patient to see in half an hour.' Then, leaning forward to resume that bedside manner once more, he asked, 'Well, now, Mr Faro?'

'As I mentioned, Mr Crowe has asked for my co-operation in the Donnelly case. I am willing to give him all the help I can—but murder without a motive?' Faro shook his head. 'It seems quite illogical.'

Neill nodded eagerly. 'Indeed it does—those were my own thoughts exactly.' Pausing, he waited for Faro to continue.

'I have a feeling that often, in such cases, there may be a clue lurking in the past.'

'Indeed.'

And the doctor gave Faro an oddly shrewd glance as he asked him, 'What do you know about the murdered girl?'

Neill looked thoughtful. 'A foundling, Mr Faro.' And, replenishing Faro's drink, he sighed. 'Let's go back to the beginning, shall we?'

6

'The girl Peg came to us as a baby, a foundling left at the church home. That's all any of us ever knew about her. Not much help there, I'm afraid.'

'No idea about parents?'

Neill shook his head. 'None. Her maiden surname was Foster but that simply reflects the fact that she was fostered. If her parents had been local folk, everyone would have known.' He sighed. 'The lass grew up to be a fine young woman—bonny, hardworking, industrious, a credit to us. We were fine pleased when she married Will Donnelly.'

'What about his inheritance?'

'So you heard about that.' Neill shrugged. 'Again, shrouded in mystery—an unknown benefactor. And folks here were happy to accept his good fortune without question. I have to tell you, sir, that we accept things as they are told to us,' he said sternly. 'We take folks as they are, we don't pry into personal matters and respect privacy.' And Faro found himself listening to a repetition of what Desmond had already told him, none of it the least help in solving a murder case.

At the end he said, 'So you have no ideas, Doctor?'

'None at all.'

Faro said carefully, 'Desmond told me the girl was raped, got pregnant by the Cara boys.'

'That piece of villainy was common knowledge.' The doctor was watching him carefully now.

'I understand that she lost the child.'

Neill nodded vaguely and with a gesture of dismissal, said, 'Miscarried—a frequent occurrence in the early months.'

'Did you attend her?'

Was there a growing tension, a cautious tightening in Neill's candid manner? 'I am not sure what you mean by attend,' the doctor said, choosing his words carefully. 'Miscarriages are spontaneous—nature's way of getting rid of an unhealthy foetus.'

In Peg's case, this was very convenient, Faro thought, needing little imagination to visualise the distraught and terrified girl. And something unspoken in the doctor's manner suggested that she had been assisted out of a tragic plight. 'How did her husband react?'

Neill regarded him steadily. 'I think the lad was grateful . . . er . . . greatly relieved.' He laughed uneasily. 'Wouldn't any husband confronted with such a situation be so?' And, as if aware of Faro's suspicions, he added smoothly, 'As you no doubt know from your long experience, abortion is a criminal

55

offence. And, in Ireland, it carries the additional moral threat of hell and damnation and excommunication.'

'Quite so,' said Faro. 'What really concerns me is whether this tragic event lay behind the motive for their murder.'

The doctor shook his head firmly. 'The motive for their murder was sheer wickedness. The Cara boys were chopping down trees, probably had been drinking heavily and decided, when the Donnellys appeared, that they were trespassing. I suspect, although I will never know for sure, that Will put up a resistance and . . . and you know the rest.' he added grimly.

'From Paddy's statement, yes.'

Neill regarded him fiercely. 'You have my word, Father McNee's word—and the entire village will back them up—that what Paddy saw and told us was the truth—the murder as he witnessed it. There is no doubt in anyone's mind in Carasheen about that,' he added firmly.

Silent for a moment, Faro then asked, 'What can you tell me about the Cara family? You were their doctor, weren't you?'

Neill smiled grimly. 'Only in extremis, one might say.'

'I understand that Michael Cara met with a fatal accident.'

'Indeed, that is so.'

And, as Faro expected, the doctor

reaffirmed Desmond's story of how the sick man, a semi-invalid, had fallen downstairs.

'Did you believe it was an accident?'

The doctor frowned. 'It appeared to be, according to his sons, who found him there when they returned home in the early hours. By the time they came for me, he had been dead for several hours.' He was silent for a moment then said slowly, 'Michael drank rather too much and was partly paralysed from a stroke.'

'He had been married twice, I was told,' Faro said. 'Did you attend his first wife in her last days?'

'I did indeed. But Michael left it too late for me to do anything. He had expected an easy birth, as had been the case with the other three boys, but there were complications this time. She died and the baby too. Poor Michael was devoted to her. He was half-mad with grief.' And Faro found himself back with his own bleak memories of his beloved Lizzie's death in childbed, with the baby son, they had both longed for, stillborn beside her. After all these years, that memory could still haunt and hurt, rising as bitter as gall in his throat. Neill continued, 'Everyone thought it was the end of Michael too and we were all thankful when he came back from a visit to Dublin with a new young wife. English she was but none the worse for that. However, she never got on well with the stepsons.' He sighed. 'I'm afraid rumour ran rife when she fell to her death from an upstairs window at Cara House.'

'An accident?'

'So it appeared,' was the cautious reply. 'To be honest with you, Mr Faro, I have always had grave doubts—suspicions regarding those three young villains. But how could I point a finger at them—three boys, the eldest not fourteen years old—without breaking their father's heart once again. So I held my peace.' Again he shook his head sadly. 'But Alice's death was his death blow too. Things went from bad to worse than bad. I have often wondered, in fact, if he knew or suspected that . . . well, her death had not been accidental . . .'

It seemed appalling to Faro that anyone could sit back and do nothing about the vile situation that Neill had put into words. 'What could we do? We were—are still—a small community. Unlike the Caras, we have no authority. They were our feudal lords and Sir Michael's sons were his legal heirs in charge of the estate which gives us our living. How could we hope to put them away, lock them behind bars?' Pausing for a moment, he added significantly, 'There is always the possibility however that they will save us the trouble.'

Faro looked at him. 'Meaning?'

'To say that they don't get on as devoted brothers is putting it mildly, Mr Faro. There is constant quarrelling among them, especially bad feelings between the eldest and the youngest, Mat and Luke. I gather from one of my patients—a rich widow named Molly Donaveen—that she is being courted by two of this unholy trinity. She is old enough to be their mother but what they want is her property as it adjoins their own. She is terrified of them . . .'

As the grandfather clock's warning wheeze indicated that it was gearing itself up for another dramatic performance, Faro realised, with some reluctance, that it was time to go. Margaret stepped through from the kitchen as her husband was showing him out. 'You must come and have supper with us, Mr Faro, and bring Imogen. We rarely get a chance of seeing her these days.'

At the gate, the doctor said, 'Come any time, Mr Faro. I would dearly like to hear how your Edinburgh police would deal with a case like the one facing us here in Carasheen. And, of course, how they deal with corpses. Do they still have trouble with the bodysnatchers, like Burke and Hare?'

Faro, repeating the invitation later to Imogen, said, 'It seems that Burke and Hare, who were murderers not bodysnatchers at all, have a lot to answer for in damaging Edinburgh's reputation.'

'What else did you discover with Uncle Des this morning?' she asked.

Faro shrugged. 'There were no clues in the Donnellys' little croft and there is an awful lot about this case that makes no sense at all—although there might be a few clues to sort out in what the doctor told me.'

'So where do you go from here?'

'The next stage is that we will have to question—or rather confront—the Cara boys who have already denied all knowledge of the crime. According to your local policeman Conn, whom I have yet to meet, they asked him who would dare take the word of the village simpleton against theirs. They believe they are quite safe—as indeed they are. Even if we got them into a court of law, a judge would dismiss Paddy's evidence as that of an unreliable witness.'

'But you can't let them get away with murder,' Imogen said indignantly.

Faro's secret wish was that, in this particular case, he could do just that. He was committed to lending a hand and he was well aware of Imogen's sense of injustice and her determination that the deaths of Peg and Will should be avenged. It was a dangerous course of action that he and her Uncle Desmond had embarked on. Faro had already decided that they should be armed and he wondered if, by any chance, Desmond possessed a revolver. Guns were things he had always treated with cautious reluctance but he had to admit they had their uses, especially in their function as deterrents. Being faced with a loaded gun would be enough to keep most villains at a

60

distance and the Cara boys weren't to know that Faro had seldom in his life used one while making an arrest.

As they finished their midday meal, Imogen said brightly, 'Aaron McBeigh is here, by the way.'

Wrestling with the complexities of a forthcoming confrontation with Carasheen's unholy trinity and wondering when Dublin were to provide the promised team of police officers, Faro stared at her blankly as he tried to think who Aaron was. At his puzzled glance, she smiled. 'We met him in Heidelberg—the rich American? You must remember—he wanted to write a book.' Imogen had a bewildering number of acquaintances that Faro had briefly met and now a vague recollection of the American came to the forefront of his mind. The memory had been carefully shelved as disagreeable since this particular acquaintance seemed to have formed a passion for Imogen. At least so Faro had believed. For, whenever they had appeared in his vicinity, McBeigh had insisted on popping up with no idea of tact. He would rush across the room waving wildly, pull out a seat at their table and, undeterred by a certain lack of spontaneity in their response to his 'May I join you?', he would settle himself in their company. Faro had to admit that sometimes Imogen, woman-like, had seemed amused and flattered by his attention.

'What on earth is he doing here in Kerry?' he demanded.

A certain sharpness in the question was not lost on Imogen. She smiled and shrugged. 'The McBeighs apparently have Irish roots . . .'

And Faro remembered that the American had the nerve to claim Imogen as a long lost relative—almost!

'He's a writer too,' she said, 'and he's compiling a book about his family history.'

'Did he know you were to be here?'

Imogen looked momentarily put out, wriggled uncomfortably and said vaguely, 'He has kept in touch—through my publisher.'

'And so he turns up in Carasheen? Now there's a coincidence,' said Faro mockingly.

Imogen's eyebrows arched in a shrewd glance. 'Surely you're not jealous, Faro?' she said softly.

Faro laid a hand over hers and said, just as softly, 'Have I reason to be jealous, Imogen dear?'

As she squeezed his hand in a returning gesture that was meant to be reassuring, Faro thought of the man in Heidelberg whose boast was of being a self-made and self-educated millionaire. He had risen from a childhood of direst poverty, the child of Irish emigrants, and, when they died, he headed west and joined the gold rush in California. But striking it rich was only the beginning. To hear him talk, which he did non-stop, there wasn't anything he hadn't tackled in his forty-odd years. His life was a chronicle of fighting grizzly bears, encountering hostile Indians and serving as a sheriff's deputy in a lawless western outpost, where he had cleaned up the outlaws single-handed. It seemed now that his only remaining challenge was to win the hand of Imogen Crowe, thought Faro cynically, as he said, 'Am I to presume he is staying with your Uncle Desmond?' As he said the words, he now knew the reason for that warning glance he had intercepted from Imogen to Desmond when the latter had mentioned his American visitor.

Imogen, having braved his displeasure, smiled brightly. 'Of course.'

'And how long is he intending to stay?' Faro asked in measured tones.

Imogen frowned. 'He doesn't say. He's very interested in Daniel O'Connell. There are some letters O'Connell wrote to his father and he's promised to let me see them. They were friends. Isn't that a coincidence now?' If all this was true, Faro decided that Aaron McBeigh seemed to have access to a truly remarkable number of coincidences as, without waiting for his comment, Imogen continued, 'He's dying to meet you again. Keeps saying that the three lawmen—you, Uncle Des and himself—ought to get together and swap reminiscences over a game of poker.'

7

There followed a day of the kind of holiday activities Faro had expected and rather dreaded. It was spent meeting a bewildering number of Imogen's relatives—aunts and cousins of varying degrees of sanguinity—drinking countless cups of strong tea and consuming vast quantities of baked confections before being shunted on to the next house where the performance was repeated. At last, they said goodnight with less passion than Faro had intended since he was suffering from acute indigestion. When each hostess proudly offered her own special recipe, he felt that a refusal would not only be discourteous, it might create a sense of rivalry and family discord. ('He liked my soda scones, bread, fruitcake, etc. better than yours, Theresa's, Mary's, etc.') He had, however, learned to walk warily in other areas and became adept at evasion. He was a smiling guest who became conveniently deaf whenever the conversation inched slyly towards hints of 'tying the knot'.

Walking towards the inn, his mind drifted back to the earlier, less agreeable events of the day and he toyed with a fleeting idea that perhaps McBeigh might be a suitable person to launch against the Cara boys and lead the expedition up to Cara House. Their meeting was to be sooner than Faro had thought and was quite inevitable. The American had been lying in wait for his return and he recognised his booming heavily accented voice long before he saw him. Any hope that he might sneak upstairs to his room past the open door of Tom's snug was dashed immediately by a roar, 'Faro!' McBeigh obviously hadn't forgotten him. Rushing over, he thrust a large hand in Faro's direction. 'Great to see you again, man. Imogen has told me all about your travels.'

Faro took a moment to recover from that merciless handshake. There were not many men who had ever diminished Jeremy Faro but everything about Aaron McBeigh seemed to have that effect. He was larger than life—the hearty voice, the hearty grin under the large moustache, the close-cropped hair, the thick spectacles but, most of all, the desperation to be a friend to all the world. Faro decided sourly that this desperation was the man's worst failing and then immediately felt ashamed of such unworthy thoughts. Was he being truly unfair? Was he just jealous at finding McBeigh here in Carasheen with Imogen? These thoughts ran through his mind as he sat there, politely listening to a chronicle of rather dull events that the American had experienced since they last met in Heidelberg. He was not expected to contribute much to the conversation. Aaron had already established promising friendships with many of the customers who were happy to draw their chairs closer so as not to miss a word of the marvels of the rich American's adventures past and present. They beamed on him encouragingly while he paused to draw breath and constantly refill their glasses.

At last Faro seized an opportunity to slip away unseen and, as he climbed the rickety stairs, he was aware of the power of his rival for Imogen's affections. He felt himself reduced to being a boy in love for the first time—a ridiculous situation for a man of his mature years, a dignified retired Chief Inspector of Police. And the awful part was his secret suspicion that Imogen was enjoying basking in the rich American's attention and obvious attraction to her. What made it even worse was his air of possession towards her. Again Faro groaned inwardly. Why had he ever allowed himself to be lured to Kerry? Dreading the confrontation that lay ahead, Faro awoke to one of those rare cloudless days agleam with radiant sunshine and warmth. So beguiling was the weather in its promise that all thoughts of storms were banished into nightmare. In a world washed clean of evil, humans are persuaded to expect miracles of faith that such tranquillity will be the future pattern of their frail lives. Alas, one had only to walk up the hill to Cara House, Faro realised, to see what nonsense such faith became.

When he came down to breakfast, Desmond and Conn were already there, waiting for him and, with brief introductions, they set off up the hill. Desmond said little but frowned incessantly, occasionally tugging at his beard as if his jaw was tender. Faro wondered if Desmond also suffered from toothache. A nagging twinge, each time he ate, reminded Faro of the devilish presence of a decayed molar and he knew that the day was looming when inevitably he would find himself reclining in the dentist's chair.

He now had a chance to study Conn O'Flynn, guardian of the law in Carasheen. He was a fresh-faced lad with carrot-red hair that did nothing for a dead white skin severely threatened by acne. Faro felt compassion for the young lad who looked as if he had stepped straight from the school classroom into that smart new uniform. Conn seemed vulnerable —innocent of any world beyond Carasheen— and totally remote from the legendary hero for whom he had been named by hopeful parents—Conn of the Hundred Battles, High King of Ireland, who had been changed into a swan by his jealous stepmother. This noble young Conn's resemblance lay more with fledgling cygnet than High King and, as the Cara's house drew nearer, he looked as if his greatest desire was to take swanlike flight across the hills and to far-away Dingle Bay.

The solid grey mansion, so imposing from the village, had arisen from the ruins of the original fortified castle, fragments of which were still visible in one wall and an untidy heap of masonry. The castle dated back to the harsh rule of Elizabeth of England and was demolished by Michael Cara's father in the 1820s. Even to one with Faro's affection for fine architecture and a tendency to regard houses as more than mere bricks and mortar, a roof and four walls to keep out the rain, the exterior of Cara House had little to commend it. Now, as they waited to be admitted, he realised valuable time had been wasted and that, before the journey had begun, they should have had a fixed plan in mind.

At last the door was opened by a lad of about ten years old. He was a thin dirty-looking urchin whose face and hands suggested only the most accidental contact with water and who was, by definition of the filthy apron about his waist, a servant. 'Who d'ye want?'

Conn stood forward, doffed his uniform helmet and said with great dignity: 'We wish to see the . . . er . . . your masters.'

The boy managed a scowl and then a nod indicating that they should follow him. Without a word, he left them inside the hall where they exchanged worried glances. Having expected something in the way of opposition, that they were expected seemed suspiciously like an ill omen and suggested that the unholy trinity boys had a story prepared. As they waited, Faro scrutinised his surroundings. The house, once so splendid, was even worse than Desmond had warned it might be. Indescribably dirty, it smelt of filth, of animals, particularly mice, of human sweat and vomit. They had to watch where they walked for there were ominous patches on the once handsome carpet where persons or animals had been very sick indeed. A staircase wound its way upwards, some of the balustrade had fallen into the hall and there were large spaces on the walls where doubtless the family portraits and landscapes, that had once held sway, had fallen and been broken or sold.

It was sickeningly like something out of the Brothers Grimm, thought Faro as the urchin returned. With a rough gesture he pushed aside a once elegant door that now was scored with cuts and deep scratches. Beyond it, the lofty panelled room with its ornate ceiling had never seen the sight of a duster or polish for many a long year. Tapestries were lost beneath dust and generations of cobwebs—a spider's paradise. Bookshelves, that had proudly housed a handsome library, the showpiece of Sir Michael Cara's grand house, had long since been abandoned and were either empty or held a gap-toothed assortment of ragged documents and empty bottles. And as for

69

those massive windows that had so impressed Faro as a convenient point from which to overlook the village, it was extremely doubtful if anything of advantage had been visible for many a year, so thick was the grime of dust and dirt.

As they waited for the notorious brothers to put in an appearance, the silence was at last broken by a loud crash and screeching voices coming from the direction of the upper hall. Voices were raised in anger. Curses were replaced by the sound of yells and blows and what sounded like china being thrown and toppling down the stairs. The noise of thin wailing children's cries, suggesting that the urchin who admitted them was not alone, then followed this commotion and the visitors concluded that these poor souls were the target of the brothers' displeasure. Faro, Desmond and Conn, representing the law of Carasheen, were stunned as they exchanged alarmed and shocked exclamations at the childish sobs. What could they do? Should they storm out and defend them? Fortunately for them, before they could make such a rash decision, the door was heaved further open and Carasheen's unholy trinity made their entrance or rather staggered in.

It was fairly obvious that, although it was not yet ten in the morning, they had already been drinking heavily. As they stood swaying slightly and contemptuously regarding the

70

newcomers, Faro was taken aback by their absolutely normal appearance. Having expected to be confronted by monsters, he instead found himself staring into the faces of three tall young men who, despite their stained and filthy clothes, had a certain attractiveness. They had the faces of angels—countenances that reminded him of the out-of-focus face of Paddy. There was a definite resemblance there. Were they perhaps related to the simple lad? It was a possibility to be investigated, Faro decided at that moment.

With mocking smiles and no words said, they stood, hands on hips, contemptuously regarding their visitors. Obviously the law of Carasheen was expected to make the first moves. And Conn did so gallantly. He stepped forward and said, 'Perhaps we have come at an inconvenient moment.' Considering the fighting they had interrupted, this was something of an understatement. 'We can return later,' he added apologetically.

No, that wouldn't do at all. Desmond touched his arm and said, 'We are here to discuss with you the recent deaths of Peg and Will Donnelly.'

One brother stood forward. 'I am Matthew Cara, the Master of Carasheen. We are aware of the Donnellys' demise.' It was the voice of authority. Faro was surprised. Desmond was to tell him later that, despite their loutish behaviour, the Cara boys had been educated in

71

English by private tutors. They had been taught to despise their native language and he doubted if they even understood it. Matthew continued, 'And what particular business is it of yours, Mr Crowe?'

'I am a policeman,' said Desmond vaguely.

It was the wrong response. Another of the lads, the youngest Faro suspected, pointed at him and jeered, 'We all know who you are, Mr Crowe. You are a retired detective from Dublin. That's who you are.'

Turning, he regarded Faro with a withering look. 'And who might this smart gentleman be? By the look of him, his roots are far from Carasheen so what is he doing in our house without an invitation? A visitor, poking into matters that do not concern him.'

'I am also a detective,' said Faro.

'You're not Irish,' shrilled Mark, the middle brother. 'That's for sure.'

'What I am is beside the point,' said Faro coldly. 'Would you please attend to the matters we wish to discuss with you?'

'Matters we wish to discuss . . .' mimicked Mark. And, turning to his brothers, he said, 'He's a spy, a rotten English spy.'

'Throw him out!' shouted Luke.

Matthew held up his hand and glared at his youngest brother. 'Hold your peace!' Then, to Conn, 'We have nothing to say regarding the unfortunate deaths of the Donnellys. We were not even in the region where they were found.'

72

Indicating his brothers in a sweeping gesture, he added, 'Is that not correct?'

Two unkempt curly heads nodded eagerly and grinned. 'We were out fishing on the lough that night, weren't we?'

'That is correct,' said Matthew. 'Since no one had the courtesy to invite us to a Carasheen wedding—it has never before been known for the Cara family to be left out.'

Faro glanced at Conn, expecting some rejoinder, but Conn was useless. He had nothing to say and, as far as the Caras were concerned, he was beneath their contempt. He might as well not have existed as he stood there frowning at the floor and biting his lip. His anxious glances towards Desmond and Faro indicated that he was leaving it to them from now on.

'We understand from a witness that you were there at the scene of the crime,' Desmond put in boldly.

'We have heard all about this "witness"—Paddy the village idiot,' said Matthew wearily and he suddenly swung round and pointed an accusing finger directly at Conn who, by this point, was trembling visibly.

'What are you here for, policeman? And why are you bringing these two . . . men to question us when we told you last time that we were not there and that a pack of lies is being told about us?'

'Besides,' put in Luke with a snigger, 'who in

73

this wide world would dare take the word of a simpleton against ours?'

'If that is all you have to say, I think you had better leave immediately and stop wasting our time,' said Matthew.

'Aye, come back when—and if—you find a better witness,' said Luke.

'Until then, jolly well leave us alone,' piped up Mark.

Their mood had changed from benign to ugly. The angel faces were lost in leering devilment. Moving forward, their manner became threatening. 'Now, get out before we throw you out.'

With as much dignity as they could summon, the representatives of the law of Carasheen made their way across the hall where Luke acknowledged Conn's unwelcome presence with a swift kick at his retreating backside. Conn swung round, fists clenched. It was a nasty moment. Desmond and Faro recognised that this was what the Caras had been waiting for. They were spoiling for a fight. Taking an arm each, Desmond and Faro seized Conn and hustled him down the steps before any further damage could be done. Their undignified exit was followed by oaths and roars of laughter from the unholy trinity as the door crashed shut behind them.

The sun was still shining outside but, to Faro, it would have seemed more appropriate if the house they had just left had been surrounded by dark and threatening clouds. 'A humiliating experience,' murmured Desmond.

'Indeed. Those children in the house—the one who let us in and his companions—who takes care of them?' asked Faro.

Conn laughed grimly. 'They are the property of the Cara brothers. Gypsy children,' he added, glad of a change of subject from the scene his two companions had witnessed. 'They ride into the encampment down by the lough, take young Romany lads, eight or ten years old, and make them work as slaves in the house.'

'Surely their parents make some resistance,' said Faro.

Conn laughed. 'Once it was a tradition. Now there is no other way of recruiting domestics since no one from the village—certainly no maids—would voluntarily work in Cara House. Just consider the fate of Peg who merely called at the door.'

'It hardly looks as if having cheap labour, or anyone at all, would make much difference to the squalor we have seen,' said Faro. 'Do the Romanies accept this vile procedure without protest?'

'They are helpless, living on Cara land on sufferance,' said Desmond. 'Granted they have done so for a hundred years—side by side with those earlier generations of Caras who would never have treated them as slaves. Romany children were employed in the house but they

75

were never maltreated—in fact, it used to be considered an honour to have one of your children work in the house. But now, if they protest or try to stop their children being taken, they will be evicted.'

'It seems that they take two or three youngsters at a time. What happens afterwards no one knows. They are never seen again. Presumably they are worked—or starved—to death,' said Conn.

'No worse, from all the accounts we hear, than many a workhouse across the water in Britain,' Desmond added grimly.

As they walked back down the hill, Faro broke the silence at last and said, 'I'm afraid that is it, then—we can do nothing more without those Dublin reinforcements.'

Desmond nodded. 'I can't understand the delay.'

'Maybe they're expecting some evidence before coming all this way,' said Conn helpfully.

'I've done all I can. They know that we have a witness.' Desmond sighed. His face was red and his voice full of suppressed anger. 'I'll get another telegraph away to them today.'

Imogen was waiting for Faro at the inn.

8

One look at Faro and the question of how it had gone died on Imogen's lips. 'I thought that wouldn't take long,' she said grimly.

Still bemused by the scene he had left and somewhat taken aback that, in the streets of Carasheen, the glorious summer morning was untarnished by the miasma they had just left, he told her briefly about the confrontation and his concern about the gypsy children. She knew about them. 'The Lees have been here almost as long as the Cara family. Even if they had wanted to evict them, there was a certain amount of reason for keeping on good terms.'

'Blackmail?' queried Faro with memories of tinkers in his own country.

Imogen laughed. 'Nothing so dramatic—just caution. The Romanies are an ancient race with their own laws, language and rules. They make a living selling baskets and the men work in the turf-cutting. The women also tell fortunes. It is said that they put a curse on the young Caras.' She shrugged. 'When all else fails, try the supernatural. But maybe their powers aren't what they used to be—this curse certainly isn't working.'

At Faro's glum expression, she took his arm and said, 'You look as if you need a change of air. I'm off to Caherciveen. It's research—I want to see Daniel O'Connell's birthplace.' Faro frowned and she said quickly, 'If you don't want to come with me, Aaron would be delighted. He's been angling to take me there since he arrived . . .'

'I thought he'd come all the way from America to find his roots.'

'He can afford it! His original reason for coming to Carasheen . . .'

'Was to see you . . .' Faro put in testily.

She smiled. 'That too, perhaps. But he was coming here to buy a pedigree Kerry bull for his ranch to breed a fine herd and remind him and everyone else of his Irish roots.'

Faro scowled and she smiled gently. 'Forget Aaron McBeigh. Let's talk of better things.' At that suggestion Faro brightened immediately. 'Tis time you saw a better face of Kerry, my darling—you've had too much of sordid local crime and intrigue.' And, indicating the handsome gig outside, she added, 'It's a tidy step so I thought we could do with something more substantial than the pony cart. Maeve made us up a picnic. Have a look at the map.'

As the horse trotted out of Carasheen and along the shores of Lough Beigh past Glenbeigh, he pointed to the spirals of smoke, the rich aroma of cooking rising into the clear air. 'The Lees' cooking fires,' she said. 'I don't know what it is they eat out there but the smell always gives me an appetite. Enjoy it, Faro, on this perfect day. This land is rich in memories of Oisin, the son of Fionn, who came back here after his long sojourn in Tir nan Og, the Land of Eternal Youth. He had left with Niamh, a golden-haired beauty he met over there on the Rossbeigh strand and went away to search for his companions in the Fianna—a band of warriors. When he came back, he did not understand that 300 years had passed while he was enchanted and that those he had left were long dead.'

As they spread a rug and ate Maeve's sandwiches and drank the red wine, the waters of the lough were ruffled by a warm breeze moving the reeds. 'Do you hear it?' Imogen said lazily.

'The breeze?'

'Nay, my love. Those are the whispers of the Celtic princesses once kept prisoners and drowned in the lough. Fancy a swim?' she laughed. 'Pity, it's time we moved on . . .'

'Your research, of course. I had forgotten.'

Leaning over she kissed him. 'Me too and it is my own fault for bringing you to an enchanted place. Diarmud, who was the foster son of the love god Aonghus Og, was also a member of the Fianna. The goddess of youth put her love spot on him, so that no woman could resist loving him.' Again leaning over, she kissed his lips firmly. 'Like that. Like you—and me,' she said softly as he drew her into his arms.

Some time later, much dishevelled but very

happy, she sat up and tidied her hair and, as she gathered up the picnic, a much happier Faro said, 'You never finished the story of Diarmud.'

'Did I not? He eloped with Grainne who was betrothed to Fionn MacCumhail and the Fianna pursued them for sixteen years. Eventually, they made an uneasy peace with Fionn who took Diarmud hunting in the forest where he was gored by an enchanted boar . . .'

'Mmm. Accident or design?'

She laughed out loud. 'The legend didn't say.' As they boarded the gig, she smiled at him and said, 'Today, this place—does it remind you . . . back in Scotland . . . another island . . . Inchmahome, wasn't it?'

He laughed. 'It was indeed. You told me the story of the Fianna that day and I never forgot it.'

'We little thought . . .' she said softly, 'did we then?'

And, looking at her with eyes of wonder, he could never have imagined what the future held for himself and an Irish terrorist, a writer who had saved his daughter Rose's life and whom he had helped to escape from Scotland—a woman who had changed his whole life. For her love, he had accepted exile from all that was once dear to him. And this was her land. Sometimes it was gentle and soft as a woman's curves, with hayricks in golden fields that were flagged by silvery stone walls and grey ribbed hills. And then there would be a dramatic change in the landscape to wild glens, with boulders like sleeping warriors and flocks of scattered sheep. Here the spread of a golden eagle's wings could be seen, hovering in the cloudless sky, while, far below its ever-watchful eyes, the turf cutters worked hard before loading their donkeys. And always, somewhere at hand, there was that glimpse of the sea, of Dingle Bay.

It was teatime before they reached Caherciveen with its memories of the great reformer who had been respected by Catholic and Protestant alike, a rare reputation in a country so fiercely Papist as Southern Ireland. There was a plaque to his memory. As they waited to be served in the tea shop of the village that was so proud of Daniel O'Connell, they were asked if they had they seen the church dedicated to his memory. After they had had tea, they visited the church and Faro watched as Imogen dipped her fingers in the holy water, crossed herself and knelt in one of the pews. He stood at the back watching her, wondering what she prayed for, speculating whether those prayers would be granted and curious to know if there was a place in them for him.

Perhaps the thought was with both of them that the day was too happy to be sullied with the dark bitterness that lay in Carasheen. Perhaps it was in both their minds, rippling below the surface of words spoken, that they should find somewhere to spend the night. It was easier than they thought. A quiet farm, just outside the village, took in visitors and stabled and fed horses. They were accepted as man and wife—no one questioned that. After a fine supper of soup and bread, they at last came to the place of the great feather bed and the snowy pillows that Faro had dreamed of. It was a night of stars in the firmament, too many to count as they looked out of the window—a night for lovers, for hearts and bodies to be united in the perfect end to a perfect day.

Fortified by a hearty farm breakfast next morning, Faro handed over the modest sum asked for and they started back to Carasheen by a different route.

'So that you can enjoy the grand tour,' said Imogen. 'This is the road through Donaveen,' she added as they drove past a handsome house, half hidden by trees, with imposing iron gates leading down the drive.

'Who lives there?' asked Faro.

'Molly Donaveen, the richest woman in Kerry.'

'The widow woman the Caras are courting?'

'The same. All you can see as far as Dingle Bay belongs to her. This is her property—it was willed to her by her husband when he died two years ago and the Cara boys are exceedingly eager to get their hands on it.'

Looking at him slyly, she said, 'She's nearer

your age than theirs. Past fifty—an artist and a good one. Looks her age, I must confess, but she was quite a beauty in her day, I'm told. Even if she was ugly as the devil, that wouldn't matter.'

'Surely past fifty is a bit old for the Cara boys?'

'Not necessarily. They aren't wanting to bed her, they just want her married to one of them so that they can have legal possession of her property.'

'Aren't there any other Donaveens?'

Imogen shook her head. 'No, alas. A childless marriage, Sean was the last of his line and there aren't—as far as we know—any living members of the family.' She sighed. 'Poor Molly, she's terrified of the Cara boys—keeps the gates locked but they jump their horses over the wall. She appealed to Conn but what could he do? What can anyone do against those young villains if she can't even lock them out? Maeve has known her for years—that's who we got the story from—and she says even her servants are deserting her now. They're terrified. The man who has been her factor was beaten up and her pet dog shot. And, if she did give in, I wouldn't rate her chances of surviving very high, once the deeds were signed.' After the scenes he had witnessed the previous morning at Cara House, Faro agreed that it was more than likely an unfortunate accident would soon befall the new Mrs Cara.

'I must take you to meet her sometime,' said Imogen as they drove back along the road towards the inn.

The weather had changed. In its strange unpredictable Irish way, yesterday's perfection seemed to have been for them alone for, the previous night, there had been a terrible storm in Carasheen and, as they were soon to discover, another death.

9

Desmond and Conn met them at the inn. 'There's been an accident,' Desmond informed them. 'One of the Cara boys—the youngest, Luke—was drowned in the lough while you were away.'

'Accident or design?' was the immediate thought that had already registered with most of Carasheen by the time Faro and Imogen arrived.

'Peter will tell you about it.'

Dr Neill was drinking a whiskey in the bar surrounded by an attentive audience of eager residents who had drifted in from their homes and surrounding farms, all avidly awaiting the details of what had happened. Faro immediately observed a certain lack of concern for the victim of this unfortunate

84

accident. In fact, he detected a general air of jubilation and heard one farmer mutter, 'The wrath of God. One less Cara to torment us.'

Women were not usually welcome in that man's domain, the public bar, but Imogen Crowe was an exception to the rule. A local heroine, who had fought for Free Ireland, Carasheen had excellent reasons to be proud of her. And, as Tom looked kindly upon her presence, it did not raise a single frown.

The doctor hailed them. He had made the discovery. 'Delivering a breech birth at a farm way beyond Donaveen, I sheltered until the worst of the thunderstorm had abated and then rode fast for home. At the lough, a riderless horse passed me on the road—a fine black beast which I guessed belonged to one of the Cara lads. Naturally I wondered what was going on so I rode along the edge of the lough. There's a bit of a hill and the path narrows—a steep slope down—you know the place . . .' Heads nodded vigorously. 'I saw a body lying face down in the water. I guessed it was one of the Cara lads and, as he wasn't moving, I guessed he had probably broken his neck when his horse threw him and had then rolled down the hill. If he wasn't dead after that, he was now almost certainly drowned.' He paused dramatically. 'I was about to go down and examine him, my professional duty, when I noticed two riders with the riderless horse. I guessed it was the brothers so I made myself scarce. I stayed out of the way—I'm not ashamed to say I hid behind a tree and watched the proceedings.'

'What if your services had been needed—if he was still alive?' asked Faro.

'They won't have anything to do with doctors. Haven't been in the house since their father died.' And, giving Faro a defiant look, added, 'So what would have happened if I had made my presence known?' No one spoke but all thoughts were the same. Knowing the black hearts of the Cara boys, the doctor would somehow have been accused of causing the accident and this would have provided yet another excuse for extending their reign of terror on Carasheen.

'Which direction were they coming from?' Faro asked.

The doctor frowned. 'Up the lough, from Donaveen way.' His sudden glance at Faro indicated that he considered the question unnecessary as he went on quickly. 'I waited until they carried him up the slope and put him over the saddle of his horse and departed. Then I rode back, collected Conn and Mr Crowe—who were both at the inn here.' This was greeted with more vigorous nods and murmured assents from those who had been present and the doctor looked towards Conn and Desmond, saying, 'We all went back to the lough.'

Conn shook his head. 'A useless journey. No

corpse and no sign of the other two Caras so there was nothing we could do.'

Considering the uncertain tempers of the brothers, Faro had no fault to find with that decision, as Desmond put in, 'We'll talk to Molly Donaveen, of course, find out if Luke was visiting her before the accident.'

'But it's a mere formality—as far as we're concerned there is no need for any enquiry,' said Conn. 'Since we have not been officially notified of any death and Dr Neill only saw him carried away . . .'

'Without a closer examination, I had no evidence that he was dead—the circumstances merely suggested that was the case,' said the doctor hastily.

'But he might have been merely injured and unconscious, is that not so?' asked Conn and the doctor agreed.

The mood, among the men gathered in the bar, indicated high hopes that Luke Cara was indeed dead—one bad penny fewer, one fewer to fear in Carasheen. That might be a desirable and satisfactory conclusion for the Cara boys' victims especially considering the deceased, perhaps the most vicious of the brothers, was hated by all. However, it seemed to Faro that, if Dr Neill was correct in his presumption of death and taking into consideration the unpopularity of Luke Cara, then there were undeniably suspicious circumstances regarding the accident. So he decided on an early visit to the scene before too many others had tramped over it.

Father McNee, having heard the news from his housekeeper, arrived at the inn where speculation was running riot. And Imogen, displaying another example of her ability to read Faro's mind, whispered, 'A trip to the lough, Faro. Not a very grand day for it, alas, but I do still have the gig.'

As they drove out of the village, Faro said, 'Presuming that the lad is dead, will there be a funeral for him?'

Imogen shook her head. 'They don't belong to the church— excommunicated long ago, I suspect, when they refused to let the priest conduct a service for their father. Everyone, good Catholics, were shocked and there are still horrendous accounts of Father McNee being thrown out.' She paused to negotiate a sharp bend in the road. 'They have a family vault belonging to the old castle which they said was good enough for the Caras—they didn't need any snivelling priest to say prayers for any of them. I think, in that case, Father McNee won't be tempted again. The only thing the folks here will be regretting is the lost opportunity for a wake,' she added cynically. Faro was silent and she asked, 'Having doubts about it being an accident or is that just the policeman in you coming out?'

Faro smiled. 'I'll tell you what I think when we reach the lough.' As the road rose sharply above the water, Faro said, 'I'll get out here and walk. No, don't drive after me. I want to look at the road on foot.'

In the muddy aftermath of the previous night's heavy downpour, there were hoof prints and also human footprints—men wearing large boots by the look of them. He looked down the slope. The reeds and grass were disturbed in a rough line down to the lough, consistent with a body rolling down to the water's edge. Imogen was at his side. 'Have you any theories?' he asked.

'Sure now, it looks as if Dr Neill's account was right. The riderless horse—well, it threw him and, injured by the fall, he rolled down there and drowned. What's wrong with that?'

'Nothing, my dear. But let's consider—he's an excellent horseman, knows his animal well, so why did it throw him?'

Imogen frowned. 'There was a storm. Could have been thunder or lightning that scared him.'

'True. What else?'

'An engineered accident, you mean? Some human agency . . . ?'

'Exactly. And, from what we know of the Cara boys' popularity, it could have been almost anyone from the village . . .'

'Of course, everyone knew that the Caras were frequent visitors at Donaveen,' said Imogen triumphantly.

Faro was examining the grass verge. 'See

here—wheel marks. Someone other than a rider was on the road—and it looks like whoever it was moved over to let someone pass.' He looked closer. 'Not the doctor—he was on horseback. And not a large carriage either—the wheels aren't wide or deep enough. A light vehicle that the driver had taken off the road—one horse pulling, most probably, a pony cart.' Pausing, he looked up the road. 'And from the direction of Donaveen.'

'So someone pulled over to let a horseman pass . . .' said Imogen.

'Or not to let him pass,' said Faro. 'This individual might have had a quite different intention—to give Luke Cara's horse the fright of its life so that it reared and threw him off. And we are presuming it was a "he",' he added thoughtfully and smiled at her. 'As I recall, females also drive pony carts in Carasheen. Like yourself.'

'And many others.' Imogen looked at him shrewdly as he led the way back to the gig.

Helping her aboard, he said, 'I think this would be an opportune moment for that introduction to the Widow of Donaveen that you promised me.'

*   *   *

There was no problem with admission. Imogen had visited before and the lodge keeper, an ancient man, bent in the back and unsteady on the legs, puffed and blew as he doffed his cap and opened the gates for them. On closer acquaintance, the house was as impressive as it had looked from a distance. The woman who opened the door and greeted Imogen so warmly was the housekeeper Annie who had been with her mistress from the day she came to Donaveen as a bride. She politely informed them that, yes, the mistress would see them.

It was a fine house on the outside and it was splendid too on the inside. They were shown in to a panelled hall with a marble-tiled floor and a sweeping oak staircase with the inevitable family portraits staring down from its walls. While they waited, Imogen pointed out the painting of a pretty young woman. 'Molly as a girl,' she whispered. Faro looked more closely. He'd seen one like it somewhere . . .

'Come this way, please,' said Annie. The sitting room they found themselves in was also panelled and had great windows overlooking Dingle Bay. Tantalising vistas of the Blasket Islands lay beyond the huge vases of fresh flowers at the windowsills. The vases were set on antique tables that had come from France and Italy, hinting at exotic travels. But there were homelier touches too—two great old sofas, both well cushioned and large enough to accommodate four persons, faced each other. Between them was a large marble fireplace whose mantelpiece bore a magnificent antique

French clock modestly ticking the hours away.

There was the sound of dogs' claws on polished floors, accompanied by a woman's voice, and Molly entered behind two spaniels that rushed forward to greet the visitors. She kissed Imogen's cheek while the exuberant dogs introduced themselves to Faro and decided to give him their undivided attention. Calling them to order, Molly took Faro's hand, saying, 'So this is your young man—at last, Imogen Crowe, we are to have a sight of him.' Faro smiled, flattered by the 'young man' but telling himself that Molly was only being polite and such would have been her description of any man who accompanied an unmarried lady. He was, however, just a little put out when she donned spectacles for a closer look.

Then for a while, he was forgotten so he took the opportunity to drift over towards the window, past a huge desk with elegant crystal decanters, a large black bottle and, somewhat incongruously, a box of pills. He picked them up idly. A label indicated Dr Neill's dispensary and the date. There were photographs too—of herself, like the painting in the hall, looking young and unrecognisably slim, the wedding photograph with Sean Donaveen, some taken on their travels, one of a young man . . . Diverted by the dogs demanding his undivided interest, he patted them enthusiastically and fondled their long silky ears.

Molly was busy questioning Imogen about

the years since they had last met. She was particularly eager to know what was the fashion in Paris these days. A devotee of the ladies' journals, she greatly admired the new style of skirt and blouse with tailored coat that were soon to replace the bustle and elaborately frilled day gowns—it was certainly more suited to the modern young woman, like Imogen herself, who was emerging with the 1890s. 'You're the height of fashion, my dear,' Molly said with an appraising glance.

Imogen laughed, smoothing her skirt. 'Two of these and a selection of blouses, plain for day—like this one—and lace for evening is all I need for our travels. Hats only when strictly necessary and I find the sailor variety is much preferable to carrying a flock of birds or a fruit basket on my head. Men have no such problems,' she added and both women turned and smiled across at Faro. Indifferent to changing fashions, his basic wardrobe had long been a Norfolk jacket, serge or tweed trousers and an overcoat known as an Ulster.

Their talk moved on to Imogen's kin in Carasheen and, as this was a conversation in which he had no part, he was able to take stock of the Widow of Donaveen.

A handsome woman of ample proportions, he thought wryly, who would have made two of Imogen Crowe. Large in every direction from the top of her head, where a mass of white hair was inexpertly held and seriously lacking in the application of a hairdresser's scissors, he thought, for many years past. A smooth and rosy complexion with more than one chin, a merry expression. Yes, he concluded, as the conversation drifted back to include him again, a very attractive widow, large as a feather bed and doubtless equally as comfortable. Certainly no mate for any of the vicious Cara blackguards.

Imogen was telling her about Luke's accident. Faro listened and watched. She said nothing but her face lost its smiling look and took on a haunted expression. At the end of it, she shook her head. 'God in his mercy knows I should be sorry for a young life lost and that I should pray for his soul, but those . . . those young devils have made my life sheer hell.' And, pausing to pat the dogs, she added, 'They killed one of my darlings and beat up my factor. To be honest, if you had said all three had been drowned, I would not have shed a single tear. I would have thanked God.' And, to Faro, in case he was shocked by such sentiments, she said, 'You cannot imagine my relief, Mr Faro . . .'

'Please call him Jeremy,' put in Imogen with a smile in his direction.

The housekeeper entered with a tray—good strong tea, scones and gooseberry jam. No alcohol despite the decanters, thought Faro with an instant's regret. His look of longing towards the desk had not gone unnoticed and

Molly smiled. 'You can help yourself to something stronger from over there. But avoid the black bottle—a courting present from Luke Cara,' she added with a grimace. 'Poteen of the home-brewed variety. Dreadful stuff. I'd have thrown it in his face if I'd dared.'

'Did he bring that last night?' asked Faro.

Molly looked at him and frowned as if trying to remember. She shook her head and said slowly, 'No, not last night.' Then, addressing Annie, 'My pills, Annie.' There was some little delay about the pills as Annie wondered where they were. Faro walked over to the desk and held up the box to Molly's great relief and Annie's chiding during which time he considered that small hesitation concerning Luke Cara.

Molly was laughing. 'I have a terrible memory for taking pills.' And a terrible memory regarding Luke Cara's last visit, Faro thought. If Luke had met with a fatal accident on the way home after visiting her, then, for her own reasons, she was keeping silent about it.

'You're not ill, are you?' asked Imogen anxiously.

'Of course not, my dear. Just a touch of indigestion and Peter, who is such a good friend, makes me up some pills and brings them himself. He enjoys the excuse for having supper with me. How is he, by the way,' she asked casually as she handed Imogen a plate.

'He's very well.'

'Good, I haven't seen him for a while.'

The conversation drifted to Scotland. Molly sighed. 'Poor Sean and I were in Edinburgh the year before he died. Would you believe it? We might have met there,' she said smiling at Faro.

Imogen laughed. 'I think that would be very unlikely, unless you had been engaged in some criminal activity.' Molly frowned and stared at Faro as if seeing him in a new, less happy light.

'Not at all,' he said hastily. 'I did have another life apart from the City Police,' he added, his sharp glance in Imogen's direction acting as a reprimand for her rather tactless remark.

There was more from Molly about Edinburgh and the places further across the world that she and Sean had visited. Then it was time to go.

On the way back to Carasheen, Imogen talked amiably about Molly and what a fine woman she was but, although he made the appropriate rejoinders, Faro's attention was elsewhere. He was thinking about the date on the pill box—yesterday's date—and, if Dr Peter Neill had delivered Molly's pills personally, then he had gone to Donaveen on the same day as Luke's accident had happened. The weather had been bad that night and Donaveen was some distance away. This meant that the doctor would probably have used the pony cart with a sheltering umbrella rather than ridden a horse as he had claimed he had done. Remembering the wheel tracks near the spot where the accident had occurred, his thoughts then returned to Molly and how she had enquired after the doctor's health with her emphasis on the fact that it was some time since she had seen him. Someone was lying. Faro again remembered grimly that, in a case of murder, the person who discovered the body was often the prime suspect. Was it possible that the doctor, on his way back from Donaveen, had met Luke Cara with fatal results? And was his good friend Molly providing him with an alibi?

Something else was worrying Faro the photographs on Molly's desk. A face that he had seen somewhere before . . . And he was to encounter the poteen bottle—or one very like it—in far more sinister circumstances.

10

At the inn, an unusual buzz of voices for this time of day, when farmers should have been engaged in more productive outdoor activities, indicated that Tom's customers had not been eager to disperse. Everyone in the area now knew about Luke Cara's suspected death, the news having spread like wildfire to the outlying farms. The place was full of speculations and folk were avid to get hold of the details of what might or might not have gone on. Conn's opinion was being sought as people wanted to be sure that Luke was really dead. Glowing in his new importance as Carasheen's policeman, with his face flushed with excitement, Conn came over to greet Faro and Imogen. Nodding towards the men clustered around the bar, he said, 'I've never heard so many different versions of what might have happened.' And to Faro he added, 'Looks as if we have a team of amateur detectives ready for recruitment.'

Desmond, sitting by the window, shook his head sadly. 'The Good Lord forbid. That's something we can be doing without.' Obviously bored by all the speculations and glad of a chance to change the subject, he smiled a greeting at Imogen and Faro. 'And where have you two been?'

'We've just called on Molly Donaveen,' Imogen told him, at which he buttoned up his tunic.

'I was just going there myself as soon as I could get away from this mob. Find out if she had a visit from Luke Cara. Just as a matter of interest, of course,' he added hastily, 'there being, as yet, no official report of any death.'

'We can give you the answer to that,' said Imogen. 'He didn't.'

Faro looked at her quickly, remembering Molly's hesitation—or was it evasion—as

Conn said, 'Nevertheless, useful to have her statement to that effect. Just a routine call,' he added sternly.

Desmond winked across at Faro and, as if Conn was not at hand and listening, he commented, 'Our policeman's eagerness to visit our rich widow on official business may have less to do with a sense of duty than the fact that Molly is very liberal with her hospitality. Annie is a fine cook. Her fruit cake's a bite of heaven.'

Conn smiled shyly. 'Well, I'll be off now.'

'I'll come with you,' said Desmond.

Conn looked momentarily put out and Desmond added casually, 'Donaveen House has other attractions too. I hear that the factor has an exceedingly pretty daughter. How is the lovely Clare?'

The tide of colour that flooded Conn's face almost outdid his red hair and indicated that Desmond's remark had hit its target.

*   *   *

Imogen was to have lunch with some friends of Maeve. 'I can't get out of this,' she told Faro. 'If I know anything of these lunches they last until after three and slide imperceptibly into afternoon tea.'

Seeing his look of disappointment, she said hastily, 'I'm sure the ladies would make you very welcome. And Maeve would be pleased.

An attractive man—especially a famous one—is great value,' she added heartily. 'Your presence would certainly give the occasion a splendid boost . . .'

Faro cut short her enthusiasm. 'No, Imogen, most definitely no.'

Imogen smiled. 'Sure? You're missing a treat. I understand the menu is to be quite splendid . . .'

Faro shuddered. 'Not even ambrosia and nectar, Imogen, and your own dear presence would tempt me.'

She looked at him gravely. 'I am so sorry,' she sighed. 'Can you amuse yourself for a few hours then?'

As she leaned forward and kissed his cheek, he felt that her regret might have held a modicum of relief, knowing how bored he could be on such occasions and how she would be constantly and anxiously glancing in his direction for signs of restlessness. Besides, that remark about amusing himself was completely out of character. Imogen knew him too intimately not to be well aware that time he spent alone was never time wasted.

'Perhaps you should invite your friend Aaron to share the feast. I am sure he would be delighted to join the ladies. His adventures would enthral them.'

Faro hoped that his somewhat cynical remark did not betray his increasing dislike of the American when Imogen smiled sweetly and said, 'What a good idea.' Certain that she was joking, Faro gave her a hard look, followed by a swift kiss and then he left her.

Amusement however was far from the forefront of his mind. He decided that this would be an excellent opportunity for a second visit to the Donnellys' farm. There might be clues he had overlooked and he knew he was always better alone on such occasions. Of course, he would have enjoyed having Imogen with him but her presence would have been as distracting as Desmond's had been on that first visit. The walk up through the wood was pleasant. Unhurried, enjoying the moment, he sat down on a tree stump and lit a pipe. Birds, unoffended by the rising tobacco smoke, sang obligingly over his head and sunlight shone silver on the distant bay. On a day like this Kerry was a paradise and Faro recalled his childhood Sunday School where the missionary hymns of Reginald Heber were great favourites.

From Greenland's icy mountains,
From India's coral strand,
Where Afric's sunny fountains
Roll down their golden sand . . .

How those words had coloured his early days. The magic realms of imagination were undiminished by age. There still lurked within him unfulfilled dreams and ambitions of

101

unexplored frontiers of travel . . . And what bitter truth lay in those lines:

Though every prospect pleases,
And only man is vile.

'Vile' also spelt 'Cara' and the unpleasant task that lay ahead. Sighing, he knocked out the pipe and continued towards the cottage. The door was unlocked—as it had been before. Nothing inside had changed, the air of melancholy of two lives brutally cut short still remained and pride and dreams for a future, that was never destined to be theirs, continued to linger in the pristine newness of their possessions and the sad and empty rooms.

A past unknown and lost forever was there too and, in the hope that it would tell him a little more of why they had been murdered, Faro returned to that photograph album, taking out and turning over each of the picture postcards. Most had been collected by the young couple as souvenirs of their limited travels in Cork and Kerry and had never been mailed. They gave no clues. Several from Dublin were addressed to Peg Foster at the church home. A scrawled greeting, 'Thinking of you.' The last card, also with a Dublin postmark, was addressed to 'Mr & Mrs Donnelly'. It bore the same conventional greeting, written in the same hand, but, irritatingly, it was unsigned with no clue to the identity of this person who had remembered Peg over the years.

Faro flipped back to those few personal photographs he and Desmond had looked at. There was a space. One had been removed. He thought for a moment, recalled the image of a young man and, with a sense of triumph, memory prompted that this was the same face he had seen very recently—on Molly Donaveen's desk. What was the connection? The door was unlocked, so who had come into the house and taken the photo? And, more importantly, why? And did that action have some significance? Did it hold any vital clue regarding the murdered couple?

He must inform Desmond of this potentially important discovery.

* * *

When he called at Maeve's house, he found Imogen washing dishes from the lunch that had become tea. She was alone as Maeve was out exercising her small charges. Throwing him a tea towel, she said, 'You've just missed Desmond—he's back from Molly's. Apparently young Conn did very well—very official he was. He even confiscated that bottle of poteen we saw this morning as being illegal.' She laughed. 'As you know, Molly was keen to be rid of it. Begged him to take it away, saying it was only fit to pour down the sink. Desmond was quite outraged at the idea. Insisted that it wasn't all that bad—a lot better than some of that blended stuff you get in shops. An acquired taste, I fear.'

Drying her hands, she put her apron over the clothesline above the fireplace and said, 'I'm off to the library. They've promised me some old newspapers I need. Coming?'

As they walked down the road Faro said, 'I have to see Desmond. I'll call on him later . . .'

Just as he was about to tell her of his discovery at the Donnellys' cottage, she said, 'You'll have to wait a couple of days. Desmond's off to Dublin to see Edith . . .'

'Who is Edith?'

Imogen looked surprised. 'His wife, of course.'

'You didn't tell me Desmond had a wife.'

'Has a wife—I thought you knew.'

'I did not. As he was retired and living alone, I presumed he was unmarried or a widower.'

'Sorry. I presumed he would have mentioned it. Edith is English and she never liked Kerry. Unfortunately Kerry didn't seem to like her either and it saved the worst possible weather for whenever they came on holiday. So, when Uncle retired from the police, not unnaturally, Edith had set her heart on some warmer dryer place. But Uncle had made up his mind. He was determined to return here and Edith flatly refused to even consider it—said she would stay in their nice warm dry Dublin house where they had lived for so many years.'

'How extraordinary,' said Faro. 'There must have been very little communication between the pair of them for such a situation to arise.'

Imogen shook her head. 'I don't think there ever was very much.'

'Have they any family?'

'None. A childless marriage—perhaps that was part of the problem. And couples don't talk about that—I mean, who was to blame or why.'

She looked at Faro, guiltily aware that he wanted to marry her but that she had always taken refuge in the excuse, although it wasn't true medically, that she was too old to have children.

'I never encountered Edith for more than a short visit, a few hours at a time, so I didn't have much chance to get to know her. However, I got the impression that she was something of a social butterfly but I'm sure Uncle Des would have liked a string of bairns. Maybe that was why he always made such a fuss of me.'

On the steps of the library, a new and rather handsome sandstone building of which Carasheen was justly proud, she said, 'You know, I have a feeling that he doesn't mind her living in Dublin and just meeting occasionally. Perhaps it's the most amicable arrangement that suits them both. By the way, part of his reason for going this time, you will be interested to hear, is that he intends finding out what happened to those police reinforcements he was promised for the Donnelly murders.'

To Faro, more than two weeks without official recognition seemed an unaccountable oversight.

11

In the library, as he examined the contents of the splendid new bookshelves while Imogen chatted to the librarian, Faro's thoughts drifted back to Desmond who would now be in Dublin. He hoped that the ex-detective would seize the opportunity of seeing his onetime colleagues and stressing the urgency of immediate action. He also hoped he would inform them that, although Luke Cara's suspected demise had reduced the three suspects to two, he was no nearer to fulfilling the task they had unofficially thrust upon him—that of solving the two murders. Or was it three now? was his unspoken thought as Imogen approached. She had an air of triumph about her, having collected the newspapers which, because of her famous reputation, she was allowed to take home with her—a quite unique dispensation, he gathered, overhearing the librarian's careful instructions.

Outside Imogen chuckled, 'Did you hear that? A writer being considered a most reliable person. I wonder how many she has met—and I know a few other quite famous folk with excellent reputations who could very rapidly change her opinion.'

When she declined his polite offer to carry the bundle of newspapers, he asked wryly, 'Do I take that remark to indicate that I am included in the unreliable persons bracket?'

Imogen laughed and hugged his arm. 'Touché. Not being personally acquainted with your study in Edinburgh, I could not swear to that. But, from Vince's description of a "rats' nest" and how poor Mrs Brook was on pain of death never so much as to whisk a duster in front of the piles and piles of paper, I think our librarian might have a good point.'

Mention of Edinburgh and Vince brought a sudden shaft of homesickness. Remembering his doctor stepson's expertise in helping him solve so many murders in his long career, he remembered the dangers they had shared and wistfully thought of how much he would have loved to have him here in Kerry. And he felt a sense of pride and gratification that Vince had been one of the few to whom he had sent a postcard. He recalled how he had given his warmest greetings to Olivia and the two children and added that he was always thinking of them. Thinking of you—it was such a conventional sentiment, much used and so handy. Again memories of those other picture postcards in the Donnellys' album were aroused. There was the intriguing possibility that the anonymous sender had some intimate connection with Peg both before and after her marriage.

Imogen was saying, 'I have to collect a book from Uncle's house. He promised to give me it for my research but, in the rush to get ready for the Dublin train, he didn't have time so he said he's left it on his desk.'

Desmond Crowe's front door was unlocked. Which seemed surprising when he was to be away for a day or two. When Faro said so, Imogen laughed. 'Nobody here ever locks doors. They all trust one another and I doubt if most folk even possess keys. Most old houses, like this one, have been handed down from father to son for generations. Doubtless keys must have existed at one time—there are keyholes to prove that. But, if you examine the locks, you'll notice that the original keys must have been so enormous it would risk grievous bodily harm to carry them around in one's pocket. So presumably they were laid aside and have been mislaid or otherwise vanished through the years.'

Faro followed her across the neat hall where a large brimmed hat with a leather band and a feather held dominion over the hallstand. 'That belongs to Aaron,' she said. 'One of several belonging to his "Saviour of the Wild West" days—a special gift of one lawman to another. Alas, I cannot imagine anyone as conservative as Uncle Des wearing such a creation in Carasheen.'

The study was also neat and tidy. Files of papers, books arranged by size and, he suspected, by alphabetical order on the bookshelves hinted that the librarian would have instantly catalogued Desmond Crowe as a reliable person. One volume was slightly out of line and spoilt the symmetry. Deciding to restore Desmond's sense of order, Faro eased it out and, in doing so, a piece of card fluttered down to the floor—a photograph. Retrieving it he stared into the face of the same young man missing from the Donnellys' album.

Imogen had picked up the book and was ready to leave. 'Wait a moment,' he said, holding up the photograph.

When he told her of his morning visit and how the photo had been removed from the album, this did not have the dramatic impact he had expected. Imogen merely shrugged. 'Wasn't Uncle Des with you the first time you went there?'

'Indeed he was. We were looking at the album together and I left him with it while I went on with the search.'

Still the significance did not seem to strike Imogen. She studied it and then laughed. 'Of course, then, there's your answer. He must have decided to remove it for some reason and bring it back with him.'

'Then why didn't he mention it?'

Imogen ran a hand through her hair, an action that he had long since recognised as an indication that she thought he was making a fuss about nothing. 'He probably didn't think it important. Perhaps he forgot all about it.' It was a logical explanation but Faro thought that Desmond's failure to mention the removal of the photo was odd. Could it be connected with some private piece of investigation? Was it some information that Desmond was unwilling to share with him and Conn? Or was it merely that, having been put in charge of the case by Dublin, Desmond wanted all the glory for himself? If that unworthy thought was true, then he must be a very disappointed man.

Imogen seemed eager to study her newspapers immediately so he left her and returned to the inn. Conn was having a drink at the bar and invited him to take a glass of stout. They moved to a vacant table where Conn said he hoped that Mr Crowe's visit to Dublin would be productive and result in those police reinforcements coming back with him. Conn sounded anxious. 'It is quite extraordinary, Mr Faro. I have been sore tempted to send them a telegraph but I fear Mr Crowe would be offended by my acting out

110

of turn, so to speak. He might think that I was getting too big for my boots—or my helmet,' he added with a wry smile. Pausing to take a sip of stout, he frowned. 'What is your opinion about Luke Cara's drowning, sir?' Before Faro could form a suitable reply, he said hastily, 'Sure now, perhaps it is myself that's developing a suspicious mind but I keep wondering whether it was an accident or, knowing the feelings of folk here, did someone kill him and push his body into the lough.'

Faro had thoughts along the same lines but said, 'Murder is going to be exceedingly difficult to prove—especially as we gather from Dr Neill that his brothers removed his body before the doctor had a chance to examine it.'

Conn nodded. 'In the circumstances, no one can be certain that Luke is dead.' He sounded resentful as, emptying his glass, he replaced it thoughtfully. 'No call for a doctor or for the priest—nothing official at all. I put it to you, Mr Faro, that there could be another burial up there in the vault—without any religious committal. That's what happened with their father. It so terribly upset our priest and shocked the whole neighbourhood . . .' He frowned and then added cautiously, 'Do you think it might have a more sinister interpretation?'

Faro looked at him sharply as he continued, 'The Caras are a bad lot, devils all of them, with no love or loyalty even to each other. We were witness to that angry quarrelling, Mr Faro. Could it be that, as there was such bad blood between them—over who Mrs Donaveen would choose—and believing she favoured the youngest, Luke . . .' Pausing dramatically, he stared at Faro intently. 'Do you think that the other two might have decided to get rid of him?'

Faro thought for a moment. 'Your theory has interesting possibilities,' he said and, waiting for two more drinks at the bar, he knew full well from his experiences that fratricide was not uncommon among families with personal vendettas to settle or where inheritance was concerned.

Returning to the table, Conn thanked him and said heavily, 'On another matter, Mr Crowe has told me he is doubtful whether we will ever solve the Donnellys' murders. Have you any ideas, any action to suggest, sir?'

'As a matter of fact, I visited their house this morning,' said Faro casually.

Corn leaned forward eagerly. 'And did you find any clues?'

Faro realised he should tell the young policeman about his examination of the photo album but, in all conscience, he could not do so since the missing photograph had turned up subsequently in Desmond's house. He still considered, despite Imogen's simple interpretation, that the circumstances of the removal of the photo needed a more plausible explanation and that somehow Molly Donaveen was involved. However, he decided to remain silent until he had spoken to Desmond on his return from Dublin. Conscious of Conn's watchful gaze, he said, 'The house was unlocked. That rather disturbed me. Miss Crowe tells me that few houses even have keys to them. Is that true?'

Conn nodded. 'Sure, that is so.' At Faro's shocked expression, he grinned. 'Life in the city has made you suspicious, sir. Country folk are different.'

'Different or not, I think open doors are inviting trouble.'

Conn shook his head sadly. 'Maybe you are right, Mr Faro. Times are changing. Folk trusting one another belongs to the days before we had to deal with villains like the Cara boys. When they ride across the common, folk rush inside and close their doors. Maybe they would feel more secure if they had keys and could lock them.' Taking another sip, he added darkly, 'Even the police station is no longer treated with awe and respect. I had an intruder this afternoon.' And before Faro could do more than look surprised, he went on: 'Someone came in and stole that illegal bottle of poteen I confiscated from Mrs Donaveen this morning.'

'Was it not under lock and key?'

Conn looked uncomfortable. 'No, it was on

my kitchen bench, quite visible, I'm afraid, to anyone looking through the window,' he added regretfully and, at Faro's quizzical expression, he added, 'I had just left it there for an hour at most while I was out on my beat. I realise that, considering the important matters we have on hand, a stolen bottle of illicit whiskey hardly merits an enquiry.'

'Stealing from the police station is still a criminal offence,' said Faro.

Conn nodded. 'I agree and it makes me very uneasy. I am aware that there is quite a taste for illegal poteen here and, therefore, it could have been anyone passing by. Like Paddy who has a habit of peeping in at windows.'

'Does Paddy like poteen?'

'He does indeed,' said Conn grimly. 'Father McNee has tried to get him out of the habit since it has a very bad effect on him. He's a mild enough lad but poteen can make him quite aggressive.' Pausing, he added, 'The Caras were in the vicinity too, getting their supply of free groceries as usual. But I can't imagine them stealing what they are already known to brew illicitly at home. Bit of a mystery, isn't it?'

It was a bit of a mystery, a rather silly and inexplicable piece of stealing, and the culprit was most likely the simple Paddy. However, the combination of the missing photo and what Imogen had said about Desmond's reluctance to pour it down the sink, on Molly's advice, lurked heavily on Faro's mind—especially as it had vanished before the afternoon train left for Dublin. Had Desmond sneaked back and lifted it on his way to the railway station? Perhaps, knowing it would be wasted, he took it quite innocently as a gift for his wife or some policeman friend.

A stolen bottle of poteen seemed rather inconsequential but Faro decided that he had a lot of questions to which he required answers when Imogen's Uncle Des returned.

12

Faro was enjoying an excellent breakfast of bacon, eggs and sausages—the best he had ever tasted. Having laid aside his fork and knife, he was tackling the toast when Imogen rushed into the dining room. Waving a letter, she said, 'This morning—from my publisher. Wretched man wants to move the publication date forward by two months to fit in with an anniversary. Two months! I ask you! This really is too much.' And, sitting down opposite him, she sighed. 'But seeing I got a hefty advance as a commission—which I have now spent—I cannot but agree.' Groaning, she covered her face with her hands. 'And that's not the worst either. The worst is yet to come. Remember I was to give a talk in Dublin? It's on Friday.'

'This Friday?'

'This Friday,' she said meekly, avoiding his eyes.

'Imogen, this is Wednesday,' Faro reminded her patiently.

'I know that,' she said, throwing down the letter. 'And it's my fault. I wrote it into my diary—the dates for Dublin and Paris—but I somehow got it on the wrong page. Oh, Faro, this really is too awful,' she wailed. 'I have nothing prepared for Friday and now we'll be leaving for Paris on Tuesday.'

'Dublin shouldn't be a problem,' said Faro soothingly. 'You have given lots of talks on our travels.'

'But not on Daniel O'Connell. This is new material. There will be people at the literary society who know a lot more about him than I do. I am just at the beginning of my researches.'

Faro stretched out a hand and covered hers. 'Imogen, dear, you have been talking about the man ever since I first knew you—you must know him inside out. Your lifelong hero, isn't he?'

'I know that. But talking to you and talking in public are not quite the same, are they? And to have to prepare a paper and give a lecture—it's a very different matter.' From his own recent experience of public speaking, Faro was well aware of that. He did not envy Imogen in

116

the slightest—although he had heard her speak many times and she always made it seem quite effortless. 'There's nothing for it, Faro. I shall have to go to Derrynane House where he lived. I really ought to have at least seen it before I give my talk on the man.'

'Very well, I'll take you there.'

Imogen frowned, avoiding his eyes. 'There's a problem. I did promise Aaron—some of his family came from Waterville and it's on the way so I could hardly refuse, could I?' At Faro's suddenly tight-lipped expression, she shook her head obstinately. 'Don't you see? It would be absolutely dreadful to sneak off without saying a word. What kind of excuse could I give when he found out, especially when we've talked about it and he's so enthusiastic? I just couldn't hurt his feelings like that.'

Faro could have confessed that he had fewer scruples about Aaron McBeigh's feelings but Imogen, waiting for his reply, was looking at him so pleadingly that he felt bound to say somewhat ungraciously, 'Then we had better take him along.'

At that Imogen brightened visibly, put her arms round his neck and hugged him regardless of her close proximity to toast and jam. 'You're a darling, you are,' she whispered. 'I know he's not your favourite man but it is only for a few hours we have to put up with him. A sort of three Hail Marys because we

117

are so happy.' Are we so happy?, thought
Faro, miserably contemplating a whole day
with Aaron McBeigh.

Relief had made Imogen exuberant. 'He'll
still be at his breakfast at the doctor's.
Margaret insisted that, while Uncle Des is
away, he eats with them.' And, with a sly look,
'Who knows, maybe he has some other
engagement and won't be free to go with us
today after all?'

Perhaps not, thought Faro, his hopes rising
as they walked across the common. As they
approached Dr Neill's house, Paddy was
leaning over the garden wall, staring intently
towards the windows. Grinning at Imogen, he
seized her hand and kissed it thoroughly. 'Are
you here to see the doctor?' she asked him in
Irish as she freed herself with some difficulty.
He shook his head, blushed fiercely and went
into a largely incomprehensible explanation. 'I
gather it is his great friend Aaron he is waiting
for,' Imogen explained as the front door was
opened by the maid who had seen them
walking up the garden path.

'The doctor is out on his rounds,' she said.
'You'll need to come later if it's him you're
after.' Looking beyond them to where Paddy
was impatiently waiting, hopping from one
foot to the other, she whispered, 'That
poor soul, he's never far away—follows the
American gentleman everywhere.'

The American gentleman had heard their

voices. He rushed from the dining room and greeted Imogen like a long-lost cousin from whom he had been parted since boyhood. Finding himself included in the embrace as a long-lost friend, as Imogen quickly and neatly turned her head to avoid Aaron's assault on her cheek, Faro found such over-exuberance trying, particularly at nine in the morning.

At the mention of Derrynane House, delighted at the prospect of spending a day with his two favourite folks, as he called them, Aaron sent the maid off to hire a carriage from the nearby stables. This was to be his treat. Lunch en route, at the most flash and expensive hotel in Waterville. No need for anything as prosaic as a picnic hamper when you were the guests of Aaron McBeigh. But there was no carriage available that day—only a gig which normally carried two persons. Aaron was undefeated at the prospect. He laughed. 'I'm game for that.' And, with a flirtatious glance at Imogen which Faro did not miss, he added, 'The more the merrier and we'll sure be cosy together.'

As they emerged, Paddy ignored Imogen and Faro and had eyes only for Aaron. He followed him with dog-like devotion and, touching his sleeve, he even managed to utter some words of greeting. Faro was touched and saddened too by this almost child-like desperation to be understood. Aaron stopped, smiled and, patting his shoulder, said, 'God bless you' in the hope that Paddy understood. Soon they were on their way. Aaron seated himself in the middle and put an anchoring arm around the shoulders of his two dear friends. They were waved off quite tearfully by an alarmed-looking Paddy. Watching him helplessly shambling after them, Faro realised that no one was safe from Aaron's good works. The sight of them boarding the gig perhaps suggested to Paddy that his hero was departing for distant shores and that he would never set eyes on him again.

Sure that the American's intentions were good, Faro felt uncharitable that the man grated on him. And, he told himself, it was not just because of McBeigh's passion for Imogen which he could describe most willingly and in some detail to anyone ready to listen. Tactlessly ignoring the fact that everyone in Carasheen knew or guessed that Faro and Imogen were long-time lovers, he said to Faro, 'Knew the moment I set eyes on her in Heidelberg that this was the greatest girl I had ever met. It happens like that only once in a lifetime,' he added, pausing to look deep into Imogen's face which was conveniently close to his own. And, talking as if she wasn't present and this was an intimate conversation between two men, he leaned across and said to Faro, 'So beautiful, don't you think? That red hair, those green eyes—so Irish. I guess that would have been enough for most men. But this great young lady has something else—she is A Writer.' He paused to beam upon Imogen. 'A Writer, ma'am,' he repeated reverently, 'and we writers have to stick together.' Faro was aware that the three of them were sticking rather too closely together on a seat that was meant to comfortably accommodate only two. 'Such a great bond we share—a very great bond. As well as being Catholics, there is something else we have in common—Daniel O'Connell.' And then turning again to Faro, he said, 'The great man is quoted as saying "no political change is worth the shedding of a single drop of human blood".'

'And that was something new for the Ireland that had suffered centuries of British rule,' said Imogen.

Aaron nodded vigorously. 'Even in the last century, Catholics could not sit in parliament or hold important state offices. Did you know that they could not even own a horse worth more than £5?'

'Terrible when you think that horses are the main form of transport, especially here where everyone owns a horse,' said Imogen.

Aaron looked at Faro. 'It wouldn't worry you, of course, since you don't ride.'

Faro grimaced. 'I lived and worked in a city . . .'

Aaron's sharp nod cut him short as he interrupted, saying, 'And I would like to bet that those handsome black mares of the Cara

121

boys cost a lot more than five pounds each.'

'Life isn't all that great now but it was made intolerable for us in the old days,' said Imogen.

'Not all the British were against Home Rule,' Faro put in defensively. 'Prime Minister Pitt was a wise man and sympathetic. He was all for Catholic emancipation . . .'

'Until your silly old King George the Third said no—definitely no—and claimed it was the cause of his madness,' said Imogen derisively. 'Then the Catholics found a champion among themselves, a lawyer who founded the Catholic Association and represented the interests of the tenant farmers.'

'I remember reading that membership was one penny a month,' said Aaron. 'One penny a month and they soon had a huge fighting fund and even the support of the clergy. It was a great time for Daniel O'Connell—all of Ireland loved him, Catholic and Protestant alike could recognise the kind of man he was—the heroic leader they had been waiting for. After his victory in the Clare elections, they wanted him at Westminster and, thanks to the then Prime Minister, the Duke of Wellington . . .' And, for Faro's benefit, he added proudly, 'The Iron Duke was an Irishman born, like himself . . .'

Faro nodded. 'The Emancipation Bill was passed in 1829,' he said and Imogen looked at him, surprised but pleased, as if she hadn't expected him to be knowledgeable about

Irish politics.

'That was just the beginning of Daniel's influence,' she said, 'when tenant farmers dared to vote in opposition to their Protestant landlords.'

'He was also a liberator to the English Catholics as well, don't let us forget that,' Aaron put in.

Imogen nodded eagerly. 'Everywhere his mass meetings soared in numbers, even reaching 100,000—enormous for the time. He arranged one at Clontarf where Brian Boru defeated the Vikings. When the government banned it—always unwilling to risk violence and bloodshed to his supporters—he called it off.'

'I seem to remember that the English brought a conspiracy charge against him,' said Aaron, 'but the House of Lords, aware of his immense popularity, set aside his sentence.'

Imogen sighed. 'That also marked the beginning of the end of his influence. Sadly there was a wind of change blowing across Ireland. People were tired of being patient and started to look to violence to achieve their aims . . .'

Faro, a champion of rights all his life, decided he would have thoroughly approved of the great liberator but now the conversation turned to politics in Dublin and a passionate debate on the rights to use guns instead of words. Losing interest, Faro's attention wandered to pleasanter pastures—namely the magnificence of land- and seascape through which they were travelling.

The initial part of their journey was a repetition of that first visit with Imogen to Caherciveen, on the edge of the Ring of Kerry. Now the scenery was even more majestic. They headed eastwards along the sea roads with tantalising glimpses of Valentia Island which Imogen pointed out to Aaron as the site of the first transatlantic cable in 1858. He laughed. 'Ironic, isn't it? Folk could get in touch with New York but they tell me they couldn't communicate with Dublin which must have been very frustrating.'

Beyond Valentia the sea was iridescent jade while, nearer the shore, wild waves hit the slate-contoured cliffs where shearwaters and kittiwakes rose, screaming at their approach. At Waterville, they stopped for lunch at one of the handsome recently built hotels overlooking the sea. Fuchsias, blooming over garden walls, and palm trees, lining the promenade, hinted at exotic lands far from Ireland. As they waited to be served, Aaron embarked on tales of the small animals he had been forced to eat to survive in his gold-mining days. Although the lunch was considerably better than Aaron's rather disgusting gastronomic experiences, it was certainly not all that he had promised. The two courses of soup and fish were perfectly edible and adequate but, Faro thought secretly, the food was no better than Maeve or Tom served up every day in Carasheen and vastly more expensive. He suspected that the cost of that one meal would have settled Maeve's grocery bill for a whole week. But Aaron had clearly enjoyed playing genial host and was in a very good humour as they set off on the final part of their journey.

The bright day was looking somewhat worn and considerably cooler when the gates of Derrynane House came in sight. They were locked. A notice read, 'House and Gardens Closed'. Imogen swore in a very unladylike fashion. 'I could scream! All this way for nothing.' United for once, Faro and Aaron tried to console her. As they boarded the gig, Aaron tried to explain that it had been a very pleasant journey at least and Faro gallantly put in a word about that excellent lunch. But Imogen refused to be consoled. 'It is all right for you two but this wasn't just a pleasure excursion for me. I needed to see the house,' she groaned.

There was nothing for it but to head back the way they had come. However, their troubles weren't over. The thin sunshine had disappeared, the sky clouded over and the faint breeze became a sharp cold wind bringing with it what they most dreaded— heavy rain. Huddling under a large umbrella was quite inadequate and it quickly dawned on them that they must take shelter. Aaron came

125

to the rescue. They would stay overnight at one of those elegant hotels at Waterville which doubtless had stable and coach accommodation. Supper and three rooms were officially booked—although only two were used. Imogen and Faro soon realised that every cloud, even one bringing with it drenching rain, has a silver lining. In much better spirits, they met with Aaron at breakfast next morning and set off on the homeward journey. But they arrived back in Carasheen to find it far from the tranquil sunny scene they had left the day before.

The Cara boys had made a call.

13

Trouble was evident as soon as the gig approached the common. People were gathered in the main street. Anxious, angry faces turned towards them and Conn pushed his way out of the crowd outside the grocery store and pointed to the broken window. 'What happened?' Faro asked him.

'Need you ask! Two of the Cara boys—Mat and Mark—came down to the shop last night. It was closed. They were drunk and started demanding more whiskey. They banged on the door, shouted that it be opened for them. They needed supplies. And, when the Kellys opened the door, they threw Sam on the floor and kicked him. When Mary tried to intervene they knocked her down—broke her wrist.'

'That's dreadful,' said Imogen. 'They are both elderly—how are they now?'

Conn shook his head. 'Sam had his head split open as he fell and Mary's arm is in a sling. Dr Neill is taking care of them.'

One of the women came forward. 'What are we to do for food? They've ransacked the shop. See for yourselves—there's hardly anything left on the shelves.'

Other women came forward to add their protests. 'What are you going to do about it, Constable Conn?' demanded one, shaking a fist at him.

'Bad enough when they were taking things without paying for them—as their right. But to beat up the poor Kellys . . .'

'You'll have to do something . . .'

'That's right. This can't go on.'

'This must be stopped. We can't live our lives like this.'

'What about our children? We all know what happened to the gypsy children down the road there.'

'Ours will be the next. Just you wait and see.'

'Nobody is safe here any more.'

Faro and Imogen followed Aaron across to Dr Neill's house. The doctor was considerably shaken by the assault on the Kellys.

127

He shook his head. 'I'm concerned about Sam, he's in a bad way, his heart is none too good. Mary is stronger but they are old people who have run this store all their lives and they are both suffering from shock. They had put up with the Cara boys taking food and not paying bills just to keep peace, but after last night . . . all I can say is that no one in Carasheen is safe any more.'

'Perhaps Uncle Desmond will come back with police reinforcements,' said Imogen.

Peter Neill looked at her bleakly and said, 'I hope so.'

*   *   *

Imogen had decided, with so little time in hand, thanks to the unexpected overnight stay in Waterville, that she would leave later that day for Dublin. Faro had intended to go with her and was looking forward to the prospect of spending some time, while she was giving her talk, exploring the city he had seen so briefly on his first visit. But it was not to be. Faro's unseen enemy was at hand or, more correctly, at mouth. Its name was Toothache. It had been the bane of his personal life for many years and was liable to make its presence felt at the most unexpected and most inconvenient times. This untimely visit had been brought about by that splendid dinner in Waterville when Faro, munching on a pork chop, had hit

128

upon a bone. Part of that troublesome decayed back molar broke off and those intermittent twinges turned into a constant painful throbbing.

He had told himself on the journey back to Carasheen that he would settle it with his old cure—whiskey or oil of cloves—and, if that failed, a hot salt poultice. So, while Imogen was packing at Maeve's, Faro took out the emergency bottle of cloves which he always carried with him and asked the maid at the inn to bring him up a hot salt poultice. She smiled sympathetically. 'The toothache is it that you have? Hot salt's the best cure—one I always use myself. Always works.' He noticed that, although she was very young, in common with most of the poor, her front teeth were showing signs of decay.

Alas, in Faro's case, the cure failed. The ache got worse and became a raging agony. With the poultice against his cheek, he walked the floor, took a large glass of whiskey and was soon feeling as if death would be good. But, gallantly packing his valise for an overnight stay, he went off to meet Imogen who took one look at the scarlet side of his face and said, 'You look dreadful!'

'Thanks for your sympathy. I feel dreadful,' he groaned and, stretching out his hand for her piece of luggage, asked, 'When's our train?'

She snatched the bag from him. 'My train is

in half an hour, Faro. But this time I am going alone.'

'Of course you're not. I wouldn't think of it.'

'I am going alone,' she said firmly, 'and you are going to do something about that tooth. This must be the umpteenth time since I've known you that I've watched you go through agonies of toothache.' She paused and shook her head. 'Faro, darling, you're a big strong man yet you let a tiny piece of decayed ivory in your jaw ruin the best moments of your life.'

'I will be all right,' Faro said desperately. 'I might find a dental surgeon in Dublin.'

'And, knowing you, you might not.' Imogen shook her head. 'They tell me Peter Neill is very good as a dental surgeon too. He will do the necessary.' Dreading what that 'necessary' involved, Faro tried to protest. But Imogen was past listening. He insisted on accompanying her to the railway station but, by the time the train steamed in, he was in such agony that he knew the journey to Dublin was out of the question. Leaning out of the window, Imogen kissed his woebegone face. 'Promise to be rid of that toothache by the time I get back—that you'll see Dr Neill right away. Promise!'

And so he waved her away, knowing that she was right. He was a coward. She had not put it into as many words but the truth, they both knew, was that he had faced implacable villains single-handed, fearlessly defied death a

130

hundred times in his long career fighting crime, while his one mortal fear of having a tooth extracted remained. Squaring his shoulders, he walked determinedly in the direction of Dr Neill's house. The maid showed him into the parlour where, in a more observant frame of mind, he would have realised that he was not particularly welcome.

Besides Aaron and the doctor, Desmond was there having arrived back from his Dublin visit. At Faro's questioning look, he shook his head. He had no hopeful news to report about the police reinforcements. The head man, as he called him—the one he had sent the original telegraph to—was away this week and no one under him had the authority to issue the order. Looks were being exchanged and Faro realised that he had interrupted something. He apologised. Dr Neill laughed. 'Nothing important—Aaron is just about to show Desmond more of his expertise at poker. Isn't that so?'

Aaron smiled and produced a pack of cards from his pocket, shuffling them as only an expert could. 'Sure thing!'

'I have already suffered for my ignorance,' said the doctor, giving Faro a polite smile.

'Poker is a serious matter,' drawled Aaron.

There was a rather lengthy pause during which Faro was expected to take his departure. He was sorely tempted. He could just walk away and tell Imogen that the doctor had been too busy. He could imagine her scornfully saying, 'Playing poker!'

Aaron said, 'Thought you were off to Dublin with Imogen.'

'That was the general idea. But . . . well . . .' Again squaring his shoulders, he remembered he had made Imogen a promise and that promise must be kept. 'I was going. Look, I am sorry to interrupt you gentlemen but I wonder, Doctor, if you could . . . well, I have infernal toothache and I was wondering if you could extract it.'

Astonished at his own brave-sounding words, he saw Dr Neill at once spring to his feet. 'My dear chap, of course. You must forgive me. I hadn't realised that you were here in the capacity of a patient.' And, patting Faro's shoulder, he said, 'Of course I'll take the wretched tooth out for you. Just go into my surgery and I'll get together my instruments.' Ushering him to the door, he said in his best bedside manner, 'Through there. Take a seat. I'll be with you in a moment.' Obviously aware of Faro's apprehension, he smiled. 'No one likes having a tooth out. We're all scared of it so don't be worrying yourself. It isn't nice but it will be over in a minute and I'll give you something to ease the pain.'

It seemed to Faro, sitting in that rather sterile room with a clock ticking unnecessarily loudly at the sore side of his face, that the doctor was taking rather longer than the promised minute. Or was that his imagination as he partly longed for and partly dreaded the door opening again? At last, footsteps announced Peter Neill. Whistling cheerfully, he removed his jacket, rolled up his sleeves and put an apron around his waist. Faro regarded this transformation with some anxiety. The lack of a jacket, the rolled-up sleeves and the addition of the apron all made him look more like a butcher than a doctor. Obviously he was expecting quite a lot of blood. Dr Neill told him to open his mouth and his action of touching the offending tooth almost rocketed Faro through the ceiling.

'That hurt? I'll just rub some of this magic stuff around your gum. We'll wait a moment and then . . .'

After a few moments, the pain dulled and Faro was again tempted to spring out of the chair and say, 'That is absolutely splendid. I will come back later, when it is more convenient for you.' But there was no chance of escape. The magic stuff had made him feel rather soothed and sleepy. However, that all ended abruptly as the doctor set to work. For all he had suffered with toothache, he had never reckoned that getting rid of it could be ten times more agonising. Seconds seemed like minutes, minutes like hours of intolerable pain and he thought his whole jaw was coming away in the doctor's blood-stained hands and that he was destined to bleed to death.

Then at last, there was a sigh from the doctor as he uttered the magic words, 'That's it then—all done. A little brute! Like to see it?' The horrible object was held in front of his eyes. Faro found it a very small and rather pathetic object to have caused him such distress. Washing out his bloodied mouth into the basin obligingly held by the doctor, he was asked, 'Want it as a souvenir?'

Faro declined the offer with a shudder. Dr Neill smiled and handed him a fresh glass. 'Drink this. It will ease the pain.'

'What pain? I thought it was over.'

The doctor interpreted his look of panic and said soothingly, 'It can be rather sore and tender for a while but nothing like what you've been suffering.'

'I am heartily glad of that,' said Faro, smiling for the first time. He was hoping to have his shattered nerves soothed by a dram of whiskey but the contents of the glass were tasteless.

'When you get back to the inn, take a rest for an hour. You'll feel fine.' But, as he rose from the chair, he found that his legs were quite shaky. Dr Neill took his arm. 'There's a gig outside waiting for you.'

'I don't need a gig, Doctor. It's just a step across the common . . .'

The doctor shook his head sadly. 'You've lost quite a lot of blood and it's rather a windy day outside so I think you should take my

134

advice,' he said kindly. Holding his arm firmly, he led him outside where Faro found, to his surprise, that he was glad of a helping hand into the gig. Dr Neill waved him off, insisting on, 'That good rest now.' As he looked back, the doctor had disappeared into the house and there was no sign of Aaron and Desmond. Presumably they were too interested in their poker game to have any concern for him.

At the inn, the driver helped him down. Dr Neill had taken care of his fare and Faro staggered upstairs, feeling as if he was more than slightly drunk. He lay down on his bed fully dressed, telling himself, 'An hour's rest and I'll be fine.'

*　　*　　*

It was still daylight when he opened his eyes. As he touched his jaw, the area of the extraction was tender but he did feel much better. Perhaps if he spent another hour resting, then he would feel like getting up, having some tea and taking a walk in the fresh air. The next time he opened his eyes, it was still daylight but he was sure that he had slept and something had awakened him. He sat up and when he touched his jaw this time, he discovered that it was still tender but also that he was badly in need of a shave. Normally, he shaved every morning. How could this be?

There was a knock on the door and the

135

maid entered. 'Awake at last are you, sir? Feeling better now? There's a visitor for you. Mr Tom said it was all right, in this case, for you to see a lady in your bedroom—even if it isn't really allowed . . .' What on earth was she talking about?

Faro heard the sound of familiar footsteps, before the shadow that was behind the maid revealed itself to be Imogen. She rushed over to his bed. 'Darling, what happened to you? You look dreadful.'

Faro sat up and proudly announced, 'Had the tooth out. Did what you told me—but what on earth are you doing back so soon? Don't tell me the talk was cancelled?'

'Darling—I've been to Dublin and back again. I gave my talk and it was well received despite my misgivings.'

Faro shook his head. 'But that's impossible.'

Puzzled, she took his hands. 'I left the day before yesterday. This is Saturday.' And, shaking her head, she laughed. 'Whatever dear Peter gave you must have made you sleep for a day and a half.' Rubbing his unshaven chin, Faro sat up sharply.

'Are you sure you're all right?' asked Imogen.

Faro grinned. 'Never felt better. A sleep like that is what I've been needing all my life. "Sleep that knits up the ravel'd sleave of care" as Shakespeare so aptly put it. Dear God, I feel like Rip Van Winkle . . .'

136

Suddenly grave, Imogen said, 'Well, things have certainly moved on in Carasheen . . .'

Faro sprang towards the door and held it open. 'Tell me about it while we eat—I'm starving.'

'Faro, listen—there's been another death . . .'

'Oh, not the poor old Kellys!'

'No, I think they're fine. It's Matthew Cara this time.'

14

While Faro changed his clothes, put on a clean shirt, washed and shaved, Imogen filled in some of the details of the latest death reported by Uncle Des. From long experience, aware that he was never at his best when he was hungry, she insisted very firmly that, having starved for more than thirty-six hours, he must also eat something before going across to Dr Neill's to hear from Conn who had made the discovery late last night.

Desmond, the doctor and Aaron were seated round the table with playing cards spread out in front of them—obviously the remains of an abandoned poker game. To Faro, it felt like déjà vu—an exact repetition of the scene he had left the day before yesterday in the doctor's surgery—except that he no longer had toothache and was left with what felt like an enormous crater in his jaw where the tooth had been extracted.

Conn had followed them in. 'You've heard then that Matthew Cara is dead?' Shaking his head, he added in bewildered tones, 'You know I found him lying at the side of the lough in the early hours of this morning, just a few yards away from where Dr Neill told us Luke was lying face down in the reeds.'

Faro was curious. 'What were you doing out there so late? It's hardly on your beat, is it?'

Conn blushed and shuffled his feet. 'I had an . . . an assignation.'

Desmond laughed. 'You might as well tell them. Soon the whole village will know. Our Conn is courting the factor's daughter Clare. Her father does not approve.'

'We've been meeting in secret. He doesn't think a village policeman is good enough for his daughter,' said Conn in disgusted tones.

Desmond smiled. 'Don't give up, lad. Some of us who began as young policeman have done remarkably well. Look at Mr Faro—and me.' Conn didn't seem reassured by this information. He looked very worried.

But Faro was much more interested in Conn's version of the night's events than he was in the young policeman's love life. 'Please continue,' he said impatiently.

'It was bright moonlight as I was returning along the lough and I noticed a horse tied to a tree. I recognised it immediately as one of the

Cara horses—no one in Carasheen owns such magnificent animals—and I was puzzled, asked myself what it was doing there and where its owner was.' Pausing dramatically, he went on, 'It certainly was odd but, wary of the uncertain tempers of the Caras, I also felt a need for caution. I looked down the slope to the loch and I saw what looked like a body.' Conn took a deep breath. 'It gave me a terrible shock, I can tell you. I thought I was seeing a ghost—Luke Cara's ghost . . .' he gulped, 'and that he must be dead after all. Anyway, I knew it was my duty so I scrambled down to the lough and it was a real body, right enough—thank God. It was Matthew Cara. At first, I thought he was dead drunk. There was an empty bottle of poteen beside him and I could smell the stuff on his clothes.' He paused again and gave Faro a triumphant look. 'And this is where it was really strange. That empty bottle beside him, I am absolutely certain it was the same one I told you about—the one that was stolen from the police station.'

'Is there some difference? Could you actually tell one bottle from another?' Faro asked.

Conn shook his head and looked annoyed at this interruption. 'It was just a feeling I had that it was the same one. Don't you ever get feelings like that, sir?' he demanded. Faro nodded but failed to see the connection. One bottle of poteen must be very like another.

The obvious answer was to add that such passionate feelings as those aroused by the theft could hardly be classed as hard evidence. Conn made an impatient gesture and, looking at the three men around the table for their support, he said, 'I knew straight away that he had drunk himself to death.' And turning to Faro again, he said, 'Everyone hereabouts knows the dangers—home-brewed poteen can be lethal. Is that not so?' His final appeal included the poker-players.

Desmond and the doctor nodded vigorously. 'Quite right, Conn. Absolutely lethal.'

Aaron merely smiled. 'Never touch the stuff myself.' And, addressing Conn, he said, 'Go ahead.'

'I haven't had a lot of experience in dealing with corpses but I know the rules so I went in search of Dr Neill. Luckily, he was at home here, playing cards with Mr McBeigh and Mr Crowe.'

The doctor smiled and said wryly, 'And losing badly too. We went back in the gig with Conn . . .'

'I preferred to be outrider,' said Aaron.

'I must admit I was somewhat bewildered,' Dr Neill continued. 'According to what Conn had told us about the empty bottle, my first thoughts were to wonder why this seemingly conscienceless young villain had chosen to stop at that particular place, tie his horse to a tree and proceed to drink himself to death—and at almost the exact spot where his youngest brother had been seen lying.' He shrugged. 'Could it be remorse? And did that indicate that perhaps Luke's accident had been arranged by Matthew? Had Matthew decided to kill him out of jealousy over Molly Donaveen? Such were my thoughts before we reached the loch. We brought his body back with us in the gig. Conn had the brilliant idea of setting the horse free as none of us fancied riding it—'

Conn nodded. 'Knowing horses as I do, I was pretty certain that it would make its own way back home and it certainly needed no urging—took off like a bolt from the blue . . .'

The doctor frowned at this interruption. 'As soon as I examined the body in the surgery, I had the answer. The cause of death was evident. This was no suicide. Death was accidental—he had choked on his own vomit.'

'Where is he now?' asked Faro, 'I should like to see his body.' The glances the three men exchanged suggested that this seemed an odd and perhaps even an unseemly request.

Dr Neill smiled kindly at Faro. 'You have some medical knowledge?'

Faro shook his head and the doctor continued, 'Then I am afraid you must take our word for the cause of death—unless you wish to go up to Cara House, that is, and ask to see him.'

Obviously feeling that a reply was

unnecessary, Desmond turned to Faro and said, 'As you might imagine, the question in all our minds was who was going to tell Mark and Luke—if he was still alive—that their brother was dead.'

'I realised it was my duty,' said Conn, 'to do so.'

'And that you had a certain reluctance about it,' said Desmond testily.

'Which we all understood,' the doctor put in with a sharp look at Desmond.

'However, even as we sat and thought about the best way, we were saved. News travels remarkably fast in Carasheen and, although it was scarcely six in the morning, Father McNee had heard. Paddy, who never seems to sleep, had told him. He's always lurking outside the house looking for Aaron.' Aaron groaned at this disclosure as the doctor added, 'Paddy had seen us arrive back in the gig with our burden which we left unattended for a few minutes while we went into the house to prepare things for an examination.'

'And, knowing Paddy's curiosity, no doubt he inspected what we had left lying under the blanket,' said Desmond grimly.

Dr Neill sighed. 'Quite frankly none of us was keen on the idea of informing Mark Cara and, when Father McNee came to ask was it true, he could see our problem and, squaring his shoulders, immediately said that he would take Matthew's body up to the house. We tried to dissuade him but not very forcefully, I must confess, and he was adamant. However he was treating this as his Christian duty. Whatever the deceased's shortcomings—and there were many . . .'

'We all agreed with him there,' Desmond put in bitterly.

Ignoring the interruption the doctor continued, 'There was a short delay while we listened to a sermon on the deceased being a human soul—one of God's creatures—and that we were to remember what the Bible told us—that no sinner was beyond Christ's redemption.'

Desmond sighed. 'None of us could think of a reply to that except that there were limits even to redemption if the father cared to look around at what had happened and what was happening to Carasheen.'

The doctor nodded. 'I had a sick old man, who was likely to die of his injuries, as well as his terrified wife, as evidence. Anyway, we were glad in our cowardly ways not to have the responsibility and Matthew was duly replaced in the gig and, with Conn at his side, representing the law, they drove up to Cara House.'

'I have to admit I was terrified. I'm a coward,' said Conn.

'Not at all,' said Faro gallantly. 'You simply aren't used to unpleasant situations which are commonplace experiences for a city policeman, I assure you.'

Desmond nodded vigorously. 'Mr Faro is right, Conn. When we are young and inexperienced, we are always scared. I know I was. I remember, to this day, my first beat on the streets in Dublin. There was a bank robbery . . .'

But Conn didn't look convinced and he interrupted, saying, 'When we got to the door with the priest and Paddy in the lead, it was opened by two of the gypsy lads. Father McNee asked to see Mark. They were gone a minute or two and came back and said Mark didn't want to see him. They were about to close the door in our faces when the father said, "Tell Mark that there has been a serious accident—involving his brother Matthew." Off they went again and I could see the father praying. They came back almost immediately and said the master had said to clear off—or words to that effect. The father was exasperated and this time said to the lads, "Tell your master that his brother Matthew is dead."' Conn paused. 'I can tell you we waited in fear and trembling after that and I was glad of the father's prayers. I thought we were going to need them. I feared that Mark would storm out—but I was wrong. We could hear whispering inside the hall and the gypsy children poked their heads round the door and said, "He says you're to sod off."' Conn shook his head. 'Poor Father McNee was shocked.

He didn't know what to do and neither did we. We couldn't take the body back to Carasheen —there would have been an uproar if he had been placed in the community hall, I can tell you. The door was still open so we carried him inside and looked around for the nearest convenient place to lay him down. There's a big carved chest, very old, against one wall so we laid him on it.'

He frowned. 'There was no still no sign of Mark or Luke or the gypsy children but I was anxious to get away. I had a nasty feeling that we were being watched from the upper landing and that, any moment, some kind of missile might land on us or a pistol might be fired. The father said some prayers and, as we left, he said loudly, so that Mark would hear, that it was now his responsibility to bury his brother's body in the family vault. When we came back down the hill, I for one was glad that the outcome had been so painless—although poor Father McNee was very distressed.' Faro listened to Conn's story very intently, his mind working not on what was being said but on the peculiarities involved in their reception by Mark Cara. That he had refused to see them, despite the tragic reason for their visit, was unaccountable—even allowing for the reputations of the three brothers. The fact that he did not choose to appear was one thing but that he was neither shocked nor surprised was quite another matter since the appearance of his brother's riderless horse must have raised some suspicions in his mind that there was something amiss. It was distinctly sinister and raised an interesting possibility. The elimination of the eldest and the youngest of the Cara brothers would have left Mark as the sole heir. So had Mark disposed of Luke and then killed Matthew in order to claim the Cara inheritance for himself?

Then there were those gypsy children to consider—the slaves and unwilling prisoners of the Cara brothers. Those undernourished and abused ten-year-olds lived in terror of their owners but it seemed utterly beyond the bounds of possibility that they could have personally been involved in luring Luke and Matthew Cara to their deaths. They could perhaps have been desperate enough to do it but they would have had neither the strength nor the ingenuity to put a plan of such magnitude into action.

And then Faro gave some thought to the gypsy encampment on the other side of the water. Had the Romanies killed two of the brothers? But that seemed completely illogical as well. It was all just speculation that did nothing to complete a baffling mystery. But then so much of the Caras' rule over Carasheen had been bizarre.

And Faro had a strange feeling that he had only heard the overture.

15

Having supper alone with Imogen, Faro was more pre-occupied than usual. He was trying to work out how he might strike out on his own and interview the gypsy children. Breaking a long silence, Imogen said, 'Those two accidental deaths. A weird coincidence, isn't it? If I didn't believe in such superstitious nonsense, I'd be inclined to think there was a curse on the Caras.' But Faro didn't believe in coincidences like this one—two of the brothers dead at almost the same spot within a few days of each other. However, according to Imogen, the folk of Carasheen had remembered an old legend and, now that it had been reawakened, it was running through Carasheen like wildfire.

'Tell me about it,' he said.

'I remember it vaguely from my childhood. My grandmother told me about a girl who had been seduced by an earlier Cara lord and she had drowned in the lough. Her mother was a witch and, after her daughter's death, she put a curse on the Cara family.'

'It has certainly taken its time to come to fruition,' said Faro who didn't believe in curses—except those that were uttered daily in moments of anger and frustration.

'Beggars can't be choosers,' said Imogen, somewhat inappropriately. 'It seems to be paying off at last—pity that it hadn't taken effect thirty years ago when a lot of the anguish of Carasheen might have been spared.'

Having been used to being called to the scene where a suspicious death had occurred, Faro was feeling aggrieved that he had been denied the opportunity of conducting his own examination. Receiving descriptions second-hand was rather like reading an unsatisfactory police report. And, whatever his feelings, he realised that, if Luke was dead, both deaths could be dismissed as accidental. One brother had been thrown from a horse and his neck had been broken—not exactly an unusual happening. The other brother had drunk too much and choked on his own vomit—again, not something that was unheard of. Such tragic events happen in normal families. Except that the Caras were not normal and nor were they remotely part of a normal family life. They were villains who lived like feudal lords, took gypsy children as slaves and lacked all human decency. As well as terrorising Carasheen, it was well known that they hated and despised each other. And it was not just because of their appalling reputations that Faro knew this—he had the evidence of his own eyes.

As for Matthew drinking himself to death because Molly Donaveen had turned him down, not in his wildest imaginings could Faro believe that any of the brothers were capable of such sentimentality. The only reason they wanted Molly's hand in marriage was because it would give them possession of her land. Love had nothing remotely to do with it. And, although Dr Neill had signed the death certificate for Matthew, Faro's suggestion regarding an inquest had been met by surprise. The doctor had laughed. 'Inquests in Carasheen! For the accidental death or suicide of one of the Caras! My dear fellow, we would have a riot on our hands!' Did the doctor also privately suspect that there was something amiss? Had he decided, in the interests of the community, to let sleeping dogs or, in this case, dead bodies lie? Whatever the cause, Faro was determined to find out the truth before Imogen's time in Kerry ran out.

*　　　　*　　　　*

Later that evening, as they walked to the high ground and watched the sun setting over the Blaskets, Imogen reminded him that their time in Carasheen was almost over and he realised that the death of Matthew Cara had put all thoughts of her Dublin visit out of his mind. When he asked her about the talk, she had told him that it went well. 'What else did you do? Was there anyone else there that you knew from previous visits?'

She frowned for a moment and then laughed. 'Oh, yes. I forgot. There was a police superintendent—a Fergus Brady—who knew you. He had been at your lecture and told me how much he enjoyed it.'

The name meant nothing to Faro—just one of an audience—but he asked, 'I presume he knew your Uncle Des?'

'Oh, yes, they had been colleagues and great friends.'

'Did he know anything about the problems back here and why that call for reinforcements had gone unanswered?'

Imogen looked at him. 'I never thought to ask.'

And when he asked, 'Had he seen Desmond on this last visit?', she sounded surprised at his question.

'I haven't the slightest idea. Why don't you ask him yourself?'

There was a pause. She shivered and said, 'Let's walk. I'm cold.'

The sunset had faded, the brilliant colours changed into a heavy bleak grey sky and, as they walked back down to the village, she changed the subject rather abruptly to travel plans for Paris. He didn't mention Dublin again and she kissed him as fondly as ever when they said goodnight. But, making his way back to the inn across the common, Faro decided that, the following day, he would talk to Desmond.

Retiring to his bed, he did not go to sleep immediately as he recalled Imogen's manner during that walk home—it was as if she had something on her mind that she did not wish to discuss with him. Was it merely the anxiety of leaving Kerry sooner than she had planned? Telling himself that it had nothing to do with Uncle Des and the Dublin visit, he consoled himself with her final words—she was going to be needing all her time, during the remainder of their stay, to complete her research on O'Connell.

She had smiled and said she hoped he would find enough to amuse himself without her. Unaware of the irony of such a remark, she had added, 'Sure and you're not to go imagining I don't love you but there are times like this when I have to be on my own. You do understand, don't you, Faro?' Watching the moonlight angle across the floor, he saw the sense in her reasoning. He was aware, during the first stages of an investigation, how necessary it was for him to be alone. Such was the present situation and he had little time left to solve this case. And solve it he would.

Far away in the clear air, the church clock struck midnight. Just a few more days and then all this would be behind him. Yawning now, he sighed. Time had always been his enemy, the implacable and undefinable enemy. And at last he slept.

*   *   *

He was saved having to go in search of Desmond. While he was at breakfast next morning, the detective hurried into the inn and greeted him genially. 'I thought this might be a good opportunity to get you alone. About Matthew Cara? Have you any new ideas that you'd like to share?' Without awaiting a reply, he continued, 'I don't know about you but I find this whole business very difficult to assess. These bizarre cases of accidental death—on almost the same spot.' He shook his head. 'Not even the slums of Dublin could have come up with anything like this. And I speak from thirty years' experience dealing with the criminal fraternity.'

'You still believe that Luke is dead and their deaths were accidents, then?'

Desmond seemed surprised by the question. 'Sure they were. What else? I was with Peter and Conn when we went down to the lough. Aaron was there too.' And, giving Faro a quick look, he added, 'I watched Peter make the examination. Matthew Cara certainly choked on his own vomit. There was plenty of evidence—anyone with a nose could smell that. And there was the spilt poteen.' After another pause, he then said apologetically, 'We would have been glad to have you there with us—as a witness—but Peter was against it. As a doctor, he realised that a patient being woken in the middle of the night was hardly the correct procedure—especially with you

152

being somewhat disabled after the tooth extraction.'

Faro shook his head. 'Drugged was closer to the mark than disabled.'

Desmond smiled. 'He hadn't bargained for his medicine taking such a prolonged effect. I suppose, like all healthy folk, your constitution got a severe shock—didn't know what had hit you.'

'A warning might have been useful. I wasn't prepared for a few hours that extended to a day and a half.'

Again Desmond gave him a comforting smile. 'I'm sure poor old Peter was surprised—and worried—by the result. I am not acquainted with his drugs for easing pain—never needed any so far myself—but even losing a day and a half is better than suffering pain. And whatever our good doctor gave you, you can be sure he meant it in your best interests.'

Faro realised there was no point in argument on the niceties of drug doses with anyone else but the doctor himself so, changing the subject, he said, 'You were saying?'

'I'm quite satisfied about the cause of Matthew's death, of course. But what is really worrying me, what I can't understand is that weird reception—the behaviour of Mark Cara refusing to see his brother's body.' He shook his head. 'It was my first thought when I woke up this morning—that there is something seriously wrong up at the house. And I don't just mean the gypsy children being kidnapped and used as slaves. He must have guessed, when the riderless horse rode in that night and Matthew didn't appear subsequently, that something was wrong.' He paused. 'If we didn't know they were accidents I would be seriously considering that he might have done away with his two brothers. As the remaining brother, he would stand to inherit. And then there was the bad blood between all three of them over Molly Donaveen.'

All this confirmed Faro's own thoughts on the matter, except for the latest accident theory which he was certain, despite the good doctor's diagnosis, was murder. For him, the smell of poteen didn't quite ring true. A less innocent doctor—one who was used to dealing with death in suspicious circumstances—would have guessed that the scene could have been rigged by the murderer to make it look as though Matthew had drunk himself to death. As for the accident involving Luke, a conveniently stormy evening, with a sudden violent noise—thunder perhaps—that made a frightened horse bolt and throw an experienced rider—that didn't quite ring true either. He said, 'I agree with you. The circumstances are certainly suspicious but I'm afraid I have nothing to add at present.'

Desmond brightened at that. 'Imogen tells

me you are both having to leave us earlier than planned. A pity—we have enjoyed your visit.'

'Did Imogen also tell you that I am determined to find the answer to quite a number of things before we go? I could do with your help.'

Desmond smiled. 'And you may have it gladly. We can put our heads together and see what Mark Cara was up to.' Then, with a sigh, he added, 'But there is so little time. Where should we start?'

'I think a visit to Molly Donaveen would not go amiss.'

'You have it. The very same thing was going through my mind,' said Desmond triumphantly. 'The Cara boys' fascination with her—or rather with her property—seems to have been the cause of two accidental deaths. If Matthew was also visiting her that evening, she was most probably the last person to see him alive.' Not quite the last—but Faro didn't bother to correct him. If his own theory was right, the last person to see Matthew alive had been his murderer on the road by the lough. Instead he asked, 'When would be an appropriate time?'

Desmond grinned. 'No time like the present. Right now—if you have finished your breakfast, that is?' Standing up, he buttoned his jacket and said, 'I'll bring the gig round.'

'Can we just drop in like this? It's only nine o'clock,' Faro asked, remembering

155

that Imogen—who was quite informal herself in her dealings with people—had heated objections to casual morning visitors.

'Sure we can,' said Desmond. 'Molly is a grand lass—a very old friend—so I am always welcome.'

'Before we go, pour yourself a cup of tea, there's plenty in the pot.' As Desmond did so, Faro produced the photograph he had found in the study, the one that had been removed from the Donnellys' album. Placing it on the table, he asked, 'Seen this before?'

With the cup halfway to his lips, Desmond returned it to the saucer and frowned. Looking bewildered, he said, 'I have. But where did you find it?'

'Between some books on a shelf in your study. I went with Imogen to collect a book you were lending her and, as I was thumbing through your splendid library, it fell out . . .' As Faro was talking, he watched Desmond's change of expression.

Now holding the photo, he sighed and said, 'So that's where it was. I've hunted high and low . . .' He frowned. 'But why did you take it?'

Faro wasn't prepared to answer that question and said only, 'I was curious to know what you were doing with it. May I ask why you removed it from the Donnellys' photo album?'

Desmond spread his hands wide. 'Isn't that obvious, my dear fellow? I wanted to see if it rang any bells for me. Perhaps someone in the village, some clue to the mystery of those murders. Dear God, we have almost forgotten them, haven't we?'

'Why didn't you mention that you'd removed it at the time?'

Desmond looked bewildered and frowned again. 'Did I not? I meant to. You were searching for clues and I just put it in my pocket and forgot. So many other things at the time . . .' And, giving Faro a searching look, he added, 'I didn't think it was all that important. It was just a hunch, as I told you, that it might be someone from Carasheen—someone I might have known in the past. Someone you wouldn't have recognised anyway.' His words confirmed what Imogen had thought about the missing photo. Had Faro, in his anxiety for any clues, given a sinister interpretation to an action that had an innocent explanation? But, as they went out to the gig, he thought about how much trouble it would have saved if that so-experienced retired Inspector Crowe had mentioned it at the time or even soon afterwards.

And now a new possibility occurred to him—an unworthy thought that this might well be a case of the retired detective not wishing to share the glory of solving a local double murder with an incomer. It was the kind of human situation that was easy enough for Faro to understand. And the worrying thing was

157

that there might also be other less innocent clues that Desmond preferred to keep to himself.

It would pay Inspector Faro to be watchful and wary.

16

As they drove along the road to Donaveen, Faro asked to stop by the lough where the two Cara brothers had been found. Desmond seemed surprised by the request and protested, 'I assure you there's nothing to see.' Faro smiled grimly as he stepped down from the gig. He refrained from saying that these words should not be in a detective's vocabulary. In all his years of experience with Edinburgh City Police, he had found there was always the distinct possibility of there being something so small and apparently trivial that it had been overlooked at the scene of the crime—something that was evident only to his own sharp eyes. In this case, he was hoping to be as fortunate at this scene of crime or, as was being stoutly maintained, scene of two accidental deaths. His hopes for success lay in the very reason that, having been dismissed as accidents, he was fairly certain the area would not have been carefully searched.

Desmond remained in the gig and watched

Faro disapprovingly as he wasted their time by going carefully down the slope. 'Where?' shouted Faro when he reached the water's edge and, pointing his whip, Desmond indicated the spot where Matthew's body had been found. Although Faro walked back and forth, there was nothing to see which might be construed as evidence of violent death and all evidence of the vomit that had choked Matthew had disappeared into the reeds. 'You are sure that's where Conn found him, lying face down there?' he said returning to the road.

'Face down, yes, that's definitely what he said.' Desmond stroked his beard thoughtfully. 'I think I see what you are getting at.'

'Odd that he should choke like that. In my experience, such accidents happen only when the drunk is lying on his back.'

'Perhaps Conn moved him to make sure that he was dead. Jump aboard.'

'May I crave your patience for just a few moments more? I presume this is the area where the horse was tied to the tree.'

'I don't know where exactly but, according to Conn, it must have been nearby.'

Any remaining clues were a remote possibility—a wild chance. Watched impatiently by Desmond, who declined to join him in what he considered a fruitless search and a waste of time, Faro took a switch of a branch and began to poke about in the nearby undergrowth among the trees. 'I will only be a moment,' he shouted and, as he disappeared from Desmond's view, he could almost hear his sigh of resignation. In the surrounding area, any evidence of Matthew's horse being tied to a tree had disappeared but Faro was more fortunate with the remainder of his search beneath the trees a little away from the road. From under the weeds he unearthed a long thin rope which had been in excellent condition and was now in two pieces. It was frayed and broken in the centre as if by some violent action.

Carrying it over his arm, he returned to the gig and Desmond asked, 'What on earth have you got there?'

'I'll show you in a minute.' Taking the two ends of the rope, he laid them across the road. There was rope to spare at either end and, as he suspected, the break came in the centre of the road. He looked up at Desmond and said triumphantly, 'The perfect mantrap.' Desmond got down from the gig. 'Take one end, if you please, and tie it to the tree—yes, there. I will take the other end and hold it down here, just out of sight. And that, I think, is how Matthew Cara and his brother Luke might have met their fatal accidents.'

Desmond continued to stare at him. 'My dear fellow. I see what you mean but it's just a piece of old rope that has perhaps lain there for ages—'

'Hardly used and discarded—a new rope,' Faro corrected him, 'and look at that frayed centre—snapped with violence but surely too good to throw away. I think that this is possibly our first piece of evidence.'

'Very well,' said Desmond, boarding the gig but sounding unconvinced. 'Throw it in the back and we'll let the others see it but, I think I should warn you, your theory sounds a little far-fetched for me. Trot on!' In a more placable mood, Desmond said, 'Crimes are much easier to solve in winter snow or frost— didn't you find that in Edinburgh? Footprints and so forth don't survive long in the countryside in summer—nature here soon obliterates everything.'

Faro knew it was true as he remembered his frustration returning to the scene where the Donnellys had been murdered two weeks previously. Thinking then that he was helping to investigate two murders, he had hardly bargained for what seemed uncommonly like four! As they drove along the side of the lough, which was glittering so innocently in morning sunshine, Faro noticed smoke rising on the other side of the water. Desmond pointed with his whip. 'Cooking fires! Smell the delicious rabbit roasting!' Apart from the smoke, the gypsy encampment was securely screened off and hidden by trees. There was no other evidence of life but Faro decided that he would pay them an informal visit sometime.

When he said so, Desmond shook his head gravely. 'They don't speak English—only Romany and some Irish. You would need an interpreter.'

'In that case, what are we waiting for? Don't you see, this is an excellent opportunity to call on them.'

At first he thought Desmond was going to refuse but he gave a long-suffering sigh as he turned the gig to the right, away from the Donaveen road. As they headed along a rough track, Desmond said, 'I'm afraid it's a waste of time but, if you insist, I'll do what I can to make you understood.' Soon they were circling the far side of the lough to where a narrow opening appeared in what looked from the distance like a natural steep cliff wall. 'This was used by smugglers in the old days. They would come in from the sea and hide themselves and their illicit goods away from prying eyes. It was a natural hiding place and easily defended. Actually, this side of the lough and beyond is Cara property and it was well known that they were happy to befriend the smugglers. The Lees have lived here for a hundred years . . .'

Their approach had been observed by a small group of men who looked tough, strong and unfriendly. Desmond spoke to one of them, indicating Faro and apparently asking to see Romany Lees who suddenly appeared and pushed himself forward. He stood regarding them impassively but with a presence at once startling and impressive. He was tall, well above average height, with a mass of thick black hair that was turning grey and a weather-beaten face and heavy gold earrings. He wore expensive-looking thigh boots and a velvet coat that was at least a century out of fashion.

As Desmond began to address him in Irish, he held up a heavily beringed hand and looking at Faro directly, he said, in halting English, 'Thou hast no business with us. Thou art forbidden to cross the threshold of Romany Lees who hath nothing to say to thou.' And, with that, he turned on his heel, indicating his conversation with them was over.

Faro said to his departing figure, 'What about your children taken by the Caras? Are they not of interest?'

The Romany came forward, his manner now threatening. Faro was over six-foot tall but Lees had the advantage in height and girth. 'What business has thou with the children of Romany Lees? Begone from our threshold, stranger. Return at your peril,' he added, drawing from his belt an old-fashioned but still villainous-looking sword.

'As you wish,' said Faro and he managed a polite bow.

Desmond was already back in the gig and Faro joined him. Eager to depart, he drove off quickly, back along the narrow track. 'I hate to say "I told you so" but I know what dealings are like with the Lees—to be avoided at all costs. And you are a stranger. They would soon recognise that and take advantage of it.'

'Don't they care about their children?' demanded Faro angrily.

'In the old days, it was traditional. Haven't you been told that two children were sent up to the big house, as they called it, as rent for the Romany site and the right to hunt on Cara grounds? They were to be servants but they were also taught to read and write. It was considered an honour. Some of them greatly benefited and went on to become leaders of the tribe—as did Lee himself. That's how he speaks that rather old-fashioned English.'

And that is how he gains a place on a fairly dubious list of suspects, thought Faro, as he said to Desmond, 'Perhaps he and his colleagues might have had their own reasons for killing Matthew Cara.'

Desmond laughed. 'Hardly! The Caras are regarded as the goose that lays the golden eggs. Don't be concerning yourself about those slave children either. I assure you there are more than enough Lees children to spare. Perhaps there were reasons why those particular two were chosen—a mother who had offended the strict Romany rules.'

'Illegitimate offspring?'

'Quite so. Unmarried or from a forbidden adulterous union.' He sighed. 'We will never learn the truth, that's for sure—or the complex rules which govern their society.' They reached the Donaveen road and climbed the steep hill to the house. And, watching Faro's withdrawn expression, Desmond added, not unkindly, 'I can only assure you without offence, my dear fellow, what is now perhaps strikingly obvious to you that we, in Carasheen, have enough to worry about and keep us busy without taking up the crusade of two ill-treated children. Much as we might deplore it on humanitarian grounds, it remains a situation we are helpless to deal with.' Having given Faro time to digest that information, he then said, 'As for that rope you found—I've been thinking that a mantrap might have distinct gypsy possibilities. There is only one drawback. It was good and strong—with plenty of life left in it. I'm pretty certain that, if they had used that new rope, they would never have thrown it away. They never let anything go to waste.'

Faro was prepared to believe that and mentally crossed the Romanies off his list. But he would be interested to see the reaction to this new piece of evidence when they got back to Carasheen. There might be someone there who regarded his discovery with more personal anxiety. And, in the words of the old proverb, 'Given enough rope, a man might hang himself.'

Molly Donaveen was not in the least put out at the impromptu appearance of two gentlemen callers at ten thirty in the morning. Her ample curves, richly corseted, were adorned by a close-fitting heavy silk dress whose many lace ruffles, as she glided across to greet them, suggested to Faro a ship in full sail. Her delighted smile and the warmest of welcomes were strengthened by the appearance of the housekeeper bearing a tray of strong tea and soda bread.

As she poured the tea, Faro made an interesting discovery. It took only minutes in the company of Molly and Desmond to suspect that they shared a close and intimate bond. Any stranger present might not have been struck by an almost unnatural avoidance of eye contact that suggested this was part of their behaviour in company—so as not to give the game away. For Faro, however, such avoidance had particular significance. It touched a personal chord for he recognised that, in the behaviour of Molly and Desmond, he was observing a situation similar to his own. This was exactly how he and Imogen behaved in strange company when they wished to keep the truth of their relationship concealed—lovers who behaved like polite but distant acquaintances.

Having made this discovery by mere chance or, as Imogen would have it, a coincidence, he could now ponder that perhaps Molly Donaveen was the real reason Edith Crowe had made her excuses and decided to remain in Dublin—thus allowing her husband to retire to Kerry alone. He was so intrigued by this new revelation, which he longed to share with Imogen, that he came back to the conversation with difficulty. However interesting this prospect, it was not the reason for their visit.

The talk, which he must somehow divert on to important matters, was still of general topics and Molly's occasional glance in Desmond's direction indicated that she wanted to know why he had brought Mr Faro with him. Although her manner towards him was warm, cheerful and hospitable, Faro, now acutely observant, felt that she occasionally revealed moments of anxiety. But he was happy to let their conversation drift past him—grateful to be able to relax in such luxurious surroundings. He admired some handsome ivory chess pieces on a table nearby and, smiling sadly, Molly said, 'Poor Sean brought them for me as a wedding anniversary present.' And, with a sigh, she continued, 'He was always going to teach me to play but the moves are far too complicated. Do you play, Mr Faro?'

'I do.'

She smiled but there was no answering invitation, had she expected one, so she added, 'Mr Crowe does not, I'm afraid.' And that denial was very odd indeed—as well as being unnecessary. Faro looked across at Desmond. He knew Desmond did play chess for he had seen a board laid out in his study. Mutely, with a trace of embarrassment, Desmond avoided Faro's eyes.

There were other pieces of bric-a-brac, small ivory figures which Molly, during a lull in the conversation, pointed out—pieces for Faro to admire—and 'poor Sean' was mentioned frequently as the donor. To a stranger, the prefix clearly indicated, if one did not know already, that her husband was deceased.

When Molly asked Faro how he was enjoying his stay in Carasheen, Desmond seized the opportunity to interrupt, saying, 'Mr Faro is interested in the Cara boys.' Molly repressed a shudder and her face, no longer smiling and calm, turned curiously old, pale and grim as Desmond added, 'You know, of course, that Matthew is dead.'

'So I have heard. The factor got it in the village this morning,' she added.

And she regarded Faro with new interest as he said, 'We are anxious to trace his movements that evening.' Her eyebrows rose and there was a trace of a smile at such formality. Faro then asked, 'Did he visit you by any chance?'

168

She laughed harshly. 'Indeed he tried to but Annie closed the door in his face. He was drunk and persistent—as usual. A horrible boy, the worst of the lot.' She shrugged. 'Candidly, I'm not sorry to know that he won't be calling on me ever again.'

'Everyone's glad for you, Molly, it must have been a terrible ordeal,' said Desmond.

Molly nodded. 'Ordeal isn't the word for it. The very idea that I could be blackmailed—I mean,' she amended hastily, 'that I would consider marrying such a creature—or his dreadful brother Luke. As I told Mr Faro here when we first met, and as the whole of Carasheen knows, I was a laughing stock, the talk of the place, being courted by lads, all rivals for my dowry, and me almost old enough to be their grandmother!' Her face looked warm now and suffused with indignation. 'I understand Mat drank himself to death—the end he richly deserved. Him and his horrible poteen.'

There was a pause and then Desmond said, 'You remember the bottle Conn confiscated on his last visit?'

'I do indeed. I told him to save the bother and pour it down the sink.'

'It was stolen from the police station and Conn believes that it was the same bottle they found lying empty beside him.'

'Then I hope someone had put poison in it first,' was the very candid reply. Desmond and

Faro exchanged looks as she continued, 'I can't help you as to whether it was the same bottle Conn took back with him or not. They often brought their wretched poteen—wanted me to drink a toast with them. They came to woo me—I think they hoped to make me drunk so that I would sign away my property as a marriage settlement.' She gave a trill of laughter as she clapped her plump hands together. 'Now wouldn't that be something? Glory be, I could have drunk the three of them under the table any day of the week, given the proper stuff and not that poisonous rubbish.'

There was more tea, some talk about Imogen's visit and no more mention of the Caras. On the way out, Faro stopped in the hall. Above the handsome console table a large unfaded patch on the wall indicated there was something missing. Faro said, 'The painting of you as a young girl—it was so lovely.'

She laughed and bowed. 'Thank you, kind sir.'

He pointed to the empty space. 'You've moved it?'

Molly shook her head vaguely. 'There was a slight accident.' Her tone indicated that she wished he hadn't drawn attention to its absence and that the question somehow embarrassed her. As Faro waited for an explanation, she sighed. 'One of the maids was dusting too vigorously—she's new to the job—

and the cord which is ancient—as I am . . .' another trill of laughter 'sure now, it just snapped. The frame broke and it's away to be repaired.'

Seeing them off at the door, she pointed to the gig and said to Desmond, 'Are you getting too grand to ride a horse these days?'

'Not at all.' A fact she must know, thought Faro, as Desmond continued, 'Mr Faro doesn't ride.'

'Me neither,' she smiled. 'Not for years. Not like the old days—since poor Sean died, I haven't had a riding horse in the stables.'

After a formal bowing and shaking of hands, the two men boarded the gig.

As Desmond drove off, he turned to Faro and said, 'Sure now, our visit has confirmed what we most needed to know. Matthew Cara was drunk when he called at the house that night. It all goes to prove that his death was an accident,' he added. Faro did not share his complacency. He was far from being convinced about that fatal accident theory. If only Molly had not made that remark about hoping the bottle of poteen had been poisoned. Could she have had a hand in it? Could the poison had been added before it left her house and Dr Neill, without any post-mortem examination, had been prepared to accept that Matthew had choked to death?

There was something else that rather disquieted Faro about that conversation. She had let slip the word 'blackmail' in connection with the Caras' wooing and, although she had amended it hastily, the remembrance of such a mistake lingered in Faro's mind. Was it possible Carasheen's 'unholy trinity' knew something vital concerning Molly—past or present—that she was anxious to hide? It had to be more than the fact, if his shrewd suspicions were correct, that she and Desmond had been or were lovers. That kind of scandal, although a little unsettling to the absent Mrs Crowe in Dublin, would have been no more than a piece of fascinating gossip in Carasheen.

Going over the interview in his mind, something regarding that missing painting was nagging at him—an urgent reason for wishing to see it again. Certain that the story about the maid's incompetence and the damaged frame had been dreamed up on the spur of the moment for his concern at its absence, he recalled her fleeting discomfiture and annoyance. Had Molly Donaveen her own reasons for removing it from the hall? But why? Evidence perhaps—but of what and why was she afraid?

As they drove along the lough shore and the place where Faro had unearthed the long rope, Desmond said, 'Perhaps we should let Conn have a look at it—if you still think it is significant.'

'I do and you are right—Conn would be the

proper person for its custody,' he said, hoping that the constable would be more scrupulous about its safety than he had been about the poteen bottle.

Nearing the common, Aaron rode over to greet them. Leaning over from his horse, he suddenly spotted the rope. 'Say, where did you gentlemen get that from?'

'I found it,' said Faro.

'Just now at the lough—near where Matthew Cara's horse was tied to the tree,' Desmond put in hastily.

Aaron didn't take his eyes off the rope. Leaning over, he seized it and said triumphantly, 'I will have you know that this belongs to me. It is my lariat and someone stole it, dammit.' Circling it over his arm, he came to the break where it fell in two parts. 'Dammit,' he repeated, examining the frayed ends. 'And they ruined it too. Best lariat I ever had—used it for roping steers, back on the ranch. Brought it with me to Europe and kept it with me on my travels—it's a part of a rider's essential equipment out West and the habit dies hard.' Smiling at them ruefully, he then said, 'Not that I expect to meet many loose steers in the streets of Heidelberg or Carasheen but it might be useful.' As he spoke, Faro guessed that someone had found it very useful indeed.

'Tell me again, Mr Faro. How did you find it?' He listened gravely, shaking his head in bewilderment with an occasional startled exclamation. Desmond remained silent—he neither confirmed nor denied Faro's theory that it had been spread across the road as a mantrap on the night of Matthew Cara's death.

With the rope in its two parts over his arm, Aaron sighed. 'You could be right, Mr Faro.' And, to Desmond, he said, 'Don't you agree, sir, that could be one answer?' Without waiting for a reply, he added, 'If we had not been with the doctor when he made his examination, I think we would be suspicious too.' And here Desmond made his contribution—a vigorous nod in agreement.

Aaron smiled. 'Whatever happened, you detectives sure are clever. But may I keep my lariat now? I'm kinda fond of it and I might need it when I'm shipping my bull back home to America.'

Looking vaguely in the direction of the house, visible through the trees, he sighed. 'I guess I shall have to go back up there and make Mark an offer. It is not a prospect I relish since I was turned down by all three of them last time but now—well, I might just be lucky.' Although Aaron had always maintained that buying the Caras' prize Kerry bull had been the reason for him coming to Carasheen in the first place, Faro had doubts about that. He was convinced that following Imogen was Aaron's real purpose and that he had been disappointed to find that she was not travelling alone. Smiling at Faro, he added, 'Like Imogen and yourself, sir, I too will be leaving at the end of the week, moving on, I guess.' He sounded regretful as he added, 'Not much time left and I shall have to see Derrynane House and tie up some unfinished family papers in Waterville again.'

Faro realised that this decision had been made fairly recently as Aaron returned to the subject of the prize Kerry bull for his ranch, to be negotiated at an exorbitant price, considering the expense and hazards of shipping such a valuable animal across to America.

'Any of you gentlemen care to accompany me to the Caras' house?' Aaron asked lightly.

He didn't sound too hopeful and seemed taken aback when Faro promptly responded, 'Of course I will.'

Aaron had provided him with exactly the excuse he needed to investigate the curious behaviour of Mark Cara.

18

Eager to share his findings with Imogen, Faro found her with a spread of papers covering the table in Maeve's sitting room. She sprang up and greeted him fondly. As he apologised for

175

disturbing her, she laughed. 'I've been writing all morning—with all that noise—so I am glad to take some time off.' As they left the house, he wondered how on earth Imogen, who was used to working in complete silence, managed to concentrate with the screams and laughter of children at play issuing from behind the closed kitchen door.

At the inn, over a ham pie and a pot of strong tea, he told her of the day's events. She seemed to accept without question the reason for the missing painting, amused at his suspicious interpretation. 'Obviously you're not used to clumsy maids, Faro darling. I'm sure your Mrs Brook was a paragon of virtue and competence but I believe Molly's story—a picture being knocked off a wall can easily happen just as she said. At least the cord didn't break of its own accord,' she added with a shudder. 'That means a death. Oddly enough, it's one of my only superstitions.'

But when he told her of his discovery of what he had thought of as a torn rope, near where the Cara brothers had been found, she was quite intrigued and did not doubt that this was the same lariat that had been stolen from Aaron. In answer to his question about it, she said, 'No, of course I haven't noticed it on his horse but then I mostly see him on foot.' As she smiled at him across the table, Faro became uncomfortably aware that Imogen could read his mind. He felt she believed that he had put a more sinister interpretation on the stolen lariat.

'I am sure he was telling you the truth,' she said gently. 'Why should he lie? These are not the actions of a guilty man, Faro. Surely, if he had been concerned in the murder of Matthew Cara—and that's what I suspect is at the back of your mind—then he would certainly not have drawn your attention to the rope you had recovered when it was lying there in the gig? My guess is that he would have ignored it completely and pretended that he had never seen it before.' Faro reluctantly had to agree that there was a certain logic in Imogen's reasoning, as she went on, 'Smart of you, though, to guess that it had been used as a mantrap. It only remains for you to find out who put it there—then you will have the proof you're looking for that Matthew Cara's death was not an accident.'

Pausing, she regarded him candidly. 'I have to tell you—warn you perhaps—that, from what I hear from Maeve, no one in Carasheen is in any rush to find his killer—if one exists. They are all more than delighted to believe that two of the unholy trinity, who have made their lives a misery, are dead and I have a horrible feeling that, once you start asking too many questions, you are not going to be very popular.' With a laugh, she took his arm and they walked out into the sunshine. 'Just as well we have only a few days left,' she said.

'Shall I take you back to Maeve's?' Faro asked.

'No, thank you. I have had quite enough for one day.' And, breathing in the warm air, she added, 'I am yours for the rest of the day. What shall we do?'

Faro had already decided that he wanted to visit the Donnelly house again. He wasn't sure whether Imogen would consider this as rather morbid but, to his surprise, she said, 'Yes, let's do that. As you say, there might still be some fragment of a clue that you and Uncle Des have overlooked. And I'm always curious about houses.'

Birds chattered above their heads as they walked through the wood, the trees swaying gently, their leaves a charming whispering canopy above their heads. 'What a pretty place,' said Imogen as they emerged at the tiny house. 'It's absolutely sweet.' The door was still unlocked and, at first glance, the interior exactly as Faro had last seen it. Except that it seemed emptier than ever and sadder too. Trapped insects buzzed against the windows where spiders were already spinning their gossamer webs. Fine motes of dust hung in the sunshine and lay thickly on the table. Scuffling sounds suggested that other more aggressive creatures than insects were taking possession. None of this worried Imogen who went from room to room and called out to him, 'How pretty! Darling—you must see this . . .'

Faro's main concern however was the photograph album which still lay in the drawer where he had found it. Taking it out, he looked again at the wedding photograph of the dead couple and, with a sense of triumph, he knew why he had wanted to return. He called to Imogen and, pointing to the photo, said: 'Does she remind you of anyone?'

Imogen squinted over his shoulder. 'Poor Peg. I only saw her once and quite fleetingly at the wedding. How sad . . .' She took it from him and looked at it tearfully. 'This house is so lovely—so happy somehow. It's still full of their dreams and hopes.'

'Have you ever seen someone who resembled Peg in Carasheen?'

Imogen thought for a moment then shook her head. 'No, but I can't claim to know the residents intimately. My visits have been very fleeting over the years.'

'Was Molly Donaveen at the wedding?'

Imogen looked at him as if this was a curious question. 'No. I'm not sure that she was invited.'

'Perhaps there was a good reason for that.'

'Why? Is it important?'

'It could be. You see, that painting I told you about—the one that met with the unfortunate accident—it could have been of Peg. It is an unmistakable likeness.'

Imogen sat down at the table and said, 'So you think Molly Donaveen was her mother, is

179

that it?'

'Almost certainly, unless she has a twin sister.'

'I don't think she has any relatives. I remember Uncle telling me how lonely she was after poor Sean died.' She sat back in a chair. 'What you are saying is quite astonishing. You realise that? But, if this is true, then it explains so many things—why Peg was given to the church house here in Carasheen as a baby, why Will had this mysterious legacy so he could buy this house.' Pausing for a moment, she added thoughtfully, 'Molly could never acknowledge Peg as her daughter—she must have been conceived and born on one of poor Sean's long voyages to South America. He was often away for two years at a time—more interested in his mines out there than his home life. It must have broken her heart not to be able to watch her baby grow up.' She regarded Faro eagerly. 'I wonder who the father was.' And then she said excitedly, 'Could it have been someone here in Carasheen?'

Pointing to the space in the photograph album, Faro said, 'There was a picture there when your uncle and I first saw the album.'

'And someone came and stole it? You realise what that means? It could have been Peg's father.'

'You're racing ahead, Imogen. Actually, your uncle took it with him. He had the same

180

thought.'

Imogen's reactions were confirming his own thoughts about the identity of the missing photograph. If Molly was Peg's mother, was that the reason the unholy trinity were blackmailing her? And suddenly the rich widow had an excellent reason for murdering the two Cara brothers. The best reason in the world for any mother—they had killed her child. She had made no secret of being glad they were dead. How she must have hated them. But how did she manage it? The more he thought of it, the more physically impossible it seemed for a woman, no longer young or very mobile, to follow them down to the lough or lie in wait—or, since she never set foot in Carasheen, steal Aaron McBeigh's lariat. He also guessed that Peg Donnelly was the reason for Molly keeping her distance from the village—there were sharp eyes that would soon have noticed such a resemblance long ago.

And, according to Dr Neill, Molly was a long-term patient. She was certainly very breathless and overweight and hadn't ridden for years. She had told them she no longer had a riding horse in the stable. On a horse, Molly would have been no match for the equestrian hard-riding of the handsome horses of the Caras. Did she have an accomplice? Perhaps it had been the factor they had beaten up— the one whose daughter Clare was in love with Conn.

Sadly or, rather, gladly Faro had to dismiss Molly as a suspect—he liked her and he had to admit that, although she might have been the brains behind the murders, she was not a suitable candidate to head the list of killers. Not by any stretch of imagination had she the right physical qualifications.

Imogen was ready to leave. While she had one last look around the house, Faro looked again at the picture postcards in the album and pocketed those with the words 'thinking of you'. Faces might change over the years but adult handwriting has characteristics that remain identifiable.

Imogen returned and, as he closed the door, she looked back and said, 'I think I might buy it, Faro. It's a dear little place and would be perfect for my visits to Carasheen. What do you think?' Faro stared at her, taken aback by the suggestion. At his hesitation, she said, 'Don't you see? It would be perfect for us—a retreat all ready and furnished.' Faro regarded the croft from the gate. 'You don't think it's a good idea,' said Imogen sadly.

'There are houses I have liked better—in France, for instance.'

'But France isn't home for me. It means nothing. But a house in Carasheen . . . it's part of my childhood.'

He put an arm around her, saying, 'Let's think about it. See if you still feel the same when we're in Paris.'

As they walked back down through the wood, he knew that, for him, the tiny house would always seem as he had first seen it—an empty, sad place, heavy with the tragedy that had overtaken its young owners and full of the melancholy of their lost hopes and dreams. He could not imagine it ever feeling like home.

'Where shall we go now?' she asked.

Faro had an idea. 'Maeve has lived here all her life, hasn't she? I've noticed a fine selection of family photos on the sideboard. Have you ever seen her photo album?' he added excitedly.

'Sure I have but . . .'

'My dear Imogen, this I think will solve our problem. There might just be something to identify our missing photo!'

*   *   *

They could not ask Maeve's permission. She was out giving the four children their twice-daily exercise but Faro sensed a certain reluctance in Imogen as she opened a drawer in the sideboard and took out a photo album. She set it on the table between them. As they leafed through, there were only a few picture postcards. This was a personal record of life in Carasheen over the past twenty years and, under each image, Maeve had conscientiously written the names of the people and the event.

183

Faro carried in his mind a clear picture of the missing photo from the Donnellys' album. Suddenly he was seeing it again. A young man standing with an arm around Maeve and, underneath, the inscription 'With Des at the Summer Fair, 1872'. 'That's him,' said Faro triumphantly.

'Uncle Des? It can't be.'

'It is—quite definitely.' And Faro knew it was the reason Desmond had removed the photo—although it was extremely unlikely that a stranger, such as himself, would recognise a stout, balding man wearing spectacles as the slim curly-haired young man of almost twenty years ago.

Imogen stared at him wide-eyed and whispered, 'The same photo you found in his study that day.' And, as realisation dawned, she sat down heavily. 'Does this mean that Uncle Desmond was Peg's father? I just can't believe it.'

'Tell me this, have you ever observed your uncle and Molly together?'

She shook her head. 'Not really.'

'Then I have—just this morning. And I made a discovery. They behave exactly as we do in the company of strangers.'

She gave him an impish look. 'You mean as if they are merely polite acquaintances?'

'Exactly.'

Imogen stood up. 'I'm quite shattered. This calls for a pot of tea.' The kettle, always at the boil, was put into action and, setting a plate of Maeve's freshly baked soda bread on the table as she poured out two cups, she said, 'Sure now and I realise this does explain a lot of things. Desmond and his wife were childless and so were Molly and poor Sean—what with him being away for long periods. So, if as you suspected this morning they are or have been lovers, then there is a strong possibility that it's true. And then there is the missing photo—of Uncle—and the fact that Peg bears a striking resemblance to Molly at the same age.' And, shaking her head vigorously, she said, 'A guilty secret kept over the years, for heaven only knows what good reasons, but it doesn't make Uncle Desmond a killer, does it?'

'I agree. It is purely circumstantial,' said Faro. 'It would never stand up in a court of law.'

She looked at him slowly. 'But it does give a lead, in your mind, that is, to why the Caras were killed?' About to take a bite of soda bread, she put it back on her plate and sighed deeply. 'There's something else—something I didn't want to tell you and hoped I could just forget all about it . . .'

19

'About my Dublin visit. I hated thinking about it and I thought if I kept it to myself then no one would be hurt,' said Imogen, 'especially Uncle Desmond.'

Faro remembered her reluctance, her tendency to change the subject when she would normally regale him with all the details of her talk, and the people she had met. 'I realised there was something wrong,' he said.

She took his hand across the table. 'What I found out still doesn't make him a killer,' she added hastily. 'You remember I told you about the detective superintendent, Fergus Brady, who had been at your lecture and how he was an old friend of Uncle Desmond?' Faro nodded and she went on, 'Uncle told me he had seen him while he was visiting Edith. But that wasn't true. Superintendent Brady said they hadn't met for a couple of years.' She paused, looking suddenly unhappy. 'But what was worse was the Dublin police knew nothing about the murder of the Donnellys and Uncle had never applied to them for reinforcements to back up the enquiry.' And, shaking her head miserably, she went on, 'The fact was that he told us all a pack of lies. I know this doesn't make him the Cara boys' killer,' she repeated quite emphatically—as if willing herself to believe it.

Faro sat back in his chair with a sigh. They were back at the beginning of it all again. The murdered couple were at the heart of all the killings and, as far as Faro was concerned, Imogen's revelations did, despite her reluctance, put Desmond at the head of the list of the suspects. One fact was becoming abundantly clear—he had already planned to avenge his daughter's death and, while he was confident that he could stay one step ahead of the village constable Conn and Inspector Faro, retired, he did not want an official police investigation complicating the issue. There was only one other complication—he had an alibi for the night that Matthew Cara was found. He was playing poker with Dr Neill and Aaron McBeigh.

'Why didn't you tell me it was a photo of your uncle as a young man?' Imogen looked uncomfortable as he added, gently, 'Didn't you recognise him?'

'Not really. You must admit he's changed a lot since that photograph was taken.' She shrugged. 'I hadn't seen him for years—I wasn't sure and I didn't think it was important.'

'That he had taken it from the photo album, you mean?' he reminded her. 'Did that not strike you as significant?'

She shook her head, evading his eyes, but Faro, watching her, knew now the depth of loyalty to one's kin in Carasheen—even though Imogen loved him, she was prepared to ignore anything which might reflect badly upon her uncle. He found himself regarding her in a new light. This was indeed a different Imogen Crowe he had discovered here in Kerry. This was the Irish girl who put her family first, based on generations of tradition, and who said, 'Be damned!' to the rest of the world and 'Be damned!' to anyone who threatened them.

There was a small unhappy silence which Faro broke by asking, 'Do you want me to go and talk to him?' Imogen looked bewildered and uncertain so he continued, 'I know you are fond of him but, if we don't find out what was behind it all, then it is going to hang over you—a wretched cloud of uncertainty. It is far better to have him put his cards—other than poker ones this time—on the table. There might be some other innocent explanation,' he added cheerfully but without much conviction.

Imogen nodded vigorously. 'You're right—as always. We have only a few days left and I couldn't bear to go away thinking . . .' She hesitated and, despite her protestations, Faro fully realised that she could not put into words the idea that Uncle Des might be a murderer. 'I won't come with you. Go on your own—whatever he has to say, it would be too embarrassing if I happened to be there.' With a promise to come back and tell her the results, Faro left her at Maeve's.

*   *   *

Walking across the common, dreading the interview that lay ahead, of bringing up the subject of why Desmond had lied to them, he half hoped that the detective would not be at home. But there he was attending to his roses in the neat little garden. Greeting Faro cheerfully, he laid aside the shears, asking, 'Time for a drink?'

'Not disturbing you, am I?'

Desmond laughed and gave him a wry look. 'You're more than welcome. I've been hoping for an excuse for a while now. I've even been known to pray for rain. I'm not much of a gardener, I'm afraid,' he added as, with a weary glance at the cloudless sky, he led the way into the house.

It was warm and pleasant in the study, a place to relax with sunlight streaming through the windows. Pouring out two generous measures of whiskey, Desmond smiled at Faro who was inspecting the books. Accepting the glass, Faro saluted him and said, 'I should congratulate you! For a man who lives alone, you are admirably tidy.' He did not add that his own untidiness drove Imogen to bouts of despair. For a man whose whole life was built on observation and deduction, she told him constantly, it certainly did not extend to his

189

personal wardrobe or his filing system.

Desmond was watching him keenly. 'Any further ideas? I was hoping you had seen signs of a breakthrough.'

Faro put down his glass. There was nothing for it but to tell him the reason for this visit. 'We were out walking and Imogen wanted to see the Donnelly house. I had another look at the photo album . . .' A shadow crossed Desmond's face as Faro continued, 'We made a discovery. The missing photo of the young man I found here in your study—it was of yourself.'

Desmond's hand on the glass trembled. He stared at Faro angrily and seemed about to deny it then, banging the tumbler down on the table, he said, 'So what difference does that make?' He blustered, 'Perhaps I just wanted it back again.'

'Then why didn't you say so? Why lie about it in the first place? Why say that you took it because you thought you might know someone in Carasheen . . .' Desmond's face reddened and, taking another drink, he evaded Faro's eyes. 'I believe that the real reason is that you did not want to be recognised. And, remembering when I first saw the painting of Molly Donaveen, I think I know why.'

Desmond turned the glass in his hand, scrutinising its contents. 'And what would that be, may I ask?'

'There was an unmistakable resemblance to

the wedding photograph in the Donnellys' album. I believe that Peg was Molly's child.' He paused. 'And I suspect that you were the girl's father.'

Desmond crashed the tumbler on to the table and sprang to his feet. 'Damn you. Damn you, Faro. What business is that of yours? Poking your nose into old history . . .'

Faro regarded him coolly. 'I take it that my suspicion is true?'

'It is and, for reasons which must be apparent even to you, it had to be kept secret. We were both . . .' he hesitated 'married to other people and were in what were apparently childless marriages. Molly did not have the best of husbands. When he was alive, he ill-used her and, although she pretends to be heartbroken at his death, her "poor Sean" routine is a bit of a sham. She was often lonely and unhappy. She was a lovely young woman,' he added wistfully and then he shrugged. 'The thing is that I loved her and still love her.'

Pausing, he looked at Faro. 'Maybe you can't understand that. Seeing us both now—changed with the years. But Molly was the one great love of my life.' He shrugged again. 'Inevitably Edith found out that we had been having an affair—although even she doesn't know about Peg.'

Faro had a sudden vision of that unwanted baby being brought up in the church home. For the child's sake, he felt the situation could

191

have been better managed. Desmond went on, 'Don't you see? The scandal would have ruined both our families. Molly would have faced Sean's wrath. He spread the rumour that she was barren—her fault not his that he had no heir. Had he known the truth he would have killed her. Being the father of an illegitimate child would have done neither my marriage nor my career much good. And I was ambitious those days. We were both desperate and I planned all sorts of schemes for Edith and I to adopt Peg—only to discover that Edith had never wanted children. She was quite happy as we were. It was quite a shock, I can tell you. All those years together and I had never known.' He walked to the window and looked across at Faro. 'I trust I can rely on your word as a gentleman to treat all this information as strictly confidential.'

'My dear fellow, your past indiscretion with Mrs Donaveen is not of the least interest to me . . .'

'Then why bother to bring it up like this?' Desmond demanded impatiently.

'Because surely you can see it has a connection with the murder of Mark Cara?'

'I don't . . .' Desmond opened his mouth and closed it again. 'Are you accusing me of killing him?' he said in heavily measured tones.

'I am only saying that you had the best reason of anyone in Carasheen—he and his

192

brothers had murdered your daughter and her husband.'

Desmond smiled mockingly. 'You will have a great deal of difficulty proving that. I have two friends, the doctor and Mr McBeigh who know and will swear that I was with them from five o'clock on the evening of Mark Cara's death and I was still there in the early hours of the morning when Conn found him.' He stood up and said, with great dignity, 'Now, if you have finished your drink and if you will excuse me, I have some letters to write.' As he watched Faro drain his glass, he added, 'Is there anything else you would like to know?'

'There is, as a matter of fact. I would really like to know why you did not apply for police reinforcements from Dublin to investigate the Donnellys' murder.'

'Of course I did . . .' Desmond began to protest but Faro held up his hand.

'I believe Superintendent Fergus Brady is an old friend and colleague of yours. Is that not so?'

'It is,' Desmond said weakly.

'Then, I have his word that you never did so——'

'You have been busy, damn you!'

For a moment, it looked as if Desmond's upraised fist was to strike Faro. He stepped back and Desmond lowered his arm in a gesture of defeat. 'You did not apply for police reinforcements and yet you told everyone in

193

Carasheen that you had done so. Surely you must realise that such an omission is capable of a very serious interpretation?'

Desmond shrugged. 'Such as?'

'That you intended to avenge the young couple's deaths by personally exterminating the Cara brothers.'

Desmond sat down heavily and leaned his elbows on the table. He shook his head. 'That was not the reason. I don't know whether you, as a retired detective, can understand this since you have such an unblemished record of success. My record has not been so successful. What Imogen doesn't know . . . what no one else here is aware of . . . is that my career ended in a failure. I bungled my last two cases in Dublin and was politely asked to retire. Even if I hadn't been personally involved, this was my last chance to prove myself, to go it alone, track down my daughter's killers, without some smart young detective from Dublin, who had wind of my past, lording it over me in Carasheen.' He paused. 'I suppose I sound like a foolish old man but, worst of all, I couldn't bear to lose face in Molly's eyes . . .'

Listening to Desmond's forbidden love brought some home truths back for Faro. He had been a widower for many years before he had met Imogen in circumstances that meant he could never have foreseen what fate had in store. Imogen had a criminal record as an Irish terrorist but she was to become the love of his life. The love of his life. His dear Lizzie seemed to belong to a different world and, had she not died in childbirth, he would have remained with her faithfully. But, as he advanced career-wise, he came to realise that they had little in common beyond Rose and Emily. Dear unsophisticated Lizzie had always known that theirs was not an ideal marriage and had hinted that he should have had someone who had more in common with him—a fact which he had hotly denied. It had taken many years for him to discover that Lizzie had been wiser than he was—it happened on the day when he knew for sure that Imogen was his true love.

Footsteps on the path outside revealed a caller—Aaron McBeigh.

So there the painful interview ended—perhaps to the relief of both Desmond Crowe and Faro.

20

The look Aaron darted at Desmond held a question. It also told Faro that the American's apologetic attitude suggested that he realised he had unwittingly stumbled into a tense atmosphere. Turning brightly to Faro, he said, 'I've been looking for you. Time for us to beard the one remaining lion in his den. And for me to make that final offer for the Kerry bull.' And to Desmond, who still looked white and shaken by the recent revelations, he said, 'Care to give us your support?'

Not surprisingly, Desmond declined and they began their walk up the hill. The faithful Paddy was not quite dogging Aaron's footsteps but remaining about twelve feet away—stopping and moving on whenever they did. Aaron shook his head, smiled kindly and seemed sympathetically disposed towards the lad. Faro had to admit that was one thing in Aaron's favour.

Staring up at the house, the American began to talk about the venture ahead and he asked, 'What have you in mind—for your part, sir?'

Faro had not thought that out very clearly. 'I simply want to see Mark Cara and ask him a few questions.'

'Do you think he'll answer them?' Aaron asked ruefully.

'I do have my doubts about whether he will cooperate. But, even if he refuses, at least I'll get a chance to make some observations and deductions.'

Aaron gave Faro a pitying look. 'That's just dandy. And I'm grateful to have you with me.'

'What do you think your chances are of getting him to part with the Kerry bull?'

Aaron was a little nonplussed by the question. 'Ever since knowing that my folks came from Kerry, it has always been my ambition to get a bull from the famous breed for my ranch.' Faro was wondering if Aaron knew what he was taking on when he added, 'I really don't know whether it will be worth it in the long run. As well as costing a small fortune to have such a valuable beast shipped across the Atlantic—if it survives the voyage better than the steerage passengers—and then halfway across America . . .'

He shrugged. 'Maybe it is just a dream that should be left as that and not dragged into a reality which, to be honest with you, now has all the makings of a nightmare.'

As they set foot on the long drive, Faro silently agreed with him. In its day, the once elegant driveway provided an imposing approach to the house. But it now sprouted a wilderness of assorted weeds and was completely overgrown. Rhododendron and fuchsia hedges had gone wild spreading tangles of branches and roots across the once neat lawns that had, in times past, been the gardeners' pride and joy. At last, the house loomed over them. Faro sighed. It had been built some seventy years ago, without imagination and with no redeeming features, to replace the more romantic but ruinous castle. Even a sunny day with a cloudless sky could not soften the harsh outlines of the ugly square building.

There were few signs of life apart from a

cloud of quarrelsome large birds hovering over a field behind the house. Raucous crows and screaming seagulls were dipping and darting over the carcass of some dead animal. A rabbit or a sheep, thought Faro, as he followed Aaron up the steps to the front door where he rang the bell. It echoed through the house. They waited. Nothing happened. Aaron frowned across at Faro and applied himself more vigorously to the bell. Again they waited. 'Where in damnation are they? That sound would wake the dead,' he said.

Faro's feeling of unease was intensifying. There was definitely something amiss. Where were the gypsy children? With an exasperated nod at Aaron, he turned the door handle. It opened. The deserted untidy hall met their gaze. It was empty of all but the sickening odours of dirt and decay Faro remembered from the last visit as he shouted, 'Is there anyone there?' They walked across the floor, their footsteps echoing hollowly. Again they called. No answer.

Aaron threw open the door of what had been the library and then tried the sitting room. Faro explored the kitchen and scullery but he hastily closed the door on the debris of past meals—the piles of dirty pots and pans and heaps of decaying food. It just remained for the upstairs to be checked. Faro heard hurried footsteps and Aaron ran down the stairs clutching a handkerchief to his nose. 'No one there. Dear God, what a place. It's a wonder they didn't die naturally of a fever. No one ever emptied the chamber pots—except on the floor.'

'What about the children?'

'No sign of them. But where the devil is Mark? Looks like he's vanished into thin air—just like his younger brother.' Aaron was already at the front door. He threw it open, saying, 'Let's get out of here before we suffocate, sir.' In the fresh air, they both drew deep breaths filling their lungs.

Paddy was sitting on a wall nearby, waiting patiently. He waved to them, smiling as if this was a social outing. Aaron waved back. 'Nothing for it, sir, but to search the outhouses. Stables first. That might give us a clue.' They hurried along the path by the side of the house. In the stables, the stalls, which had presumably housed the Cara horses, were empty. Aaron leaned down and looked at the horses' droppings and shook his head. 'These aren't new, sir. Days old.' And, with a grim smile, he added, 'An old lawman's habit, sir, first thing we check on the trail.'

Both men were glad of the gentle breeze as they stared up at the cloudless sky filled with the noisy screeching of predatory birds, the darting shapes of black and white, which seemed to have multiplied over the field. Aaron took Faro's arm. 'Carrion, sir. That's what they are,' he shouted, 'And that's where

199

the Kerry bull is kept. They showed me last time I came. God, I hope nothing has happened to the beast.' As they raced along the path, Aaron, who was younger and fleeter than Faro, drew a few steps ahead of him. Their arrival swept a cloud of angry birds into the air. A few of the bolder ones remained, cocking an eye at them as they looked up— reluctant to withdraw from their dreadful feast. Aaron gave a choking gasp as he turned to Faro. Beyond the gate, the body on the ground was not the prized Kerry bull. The body in the bullpen was that of Mark Cara. The great bleeding holes in his chest told their own dreadful story. He had been gored to death. As for the perpetrator of this crime, the Kerry bull sat calmly under a tree by the fence, at the far end of the field, munching happily with his back to the horrific scene before them, totally ignoring his victim's body.

'We'd better get back.' said Aaron. 'There's nothing we can do.' Faro, sick at the smell of blood and death, shook his head. 'There's nothing you can do,' said Aaron repeated urgently. 'You can't go over there. The man's dead. We should go and get . . .'

Faro looked up at him. 'Get help, you mean? It's a bit late for that. Besides, I think Paddy will be well ahead of us with the bad news,' he added, pointing to the wild figure who had followed them and was now racing down towards Carasheen.

'Can you make sure the beast doesn't come near while I have a look at the body?'

'You must be crazy,' said Aaron. 'He could cover those twenty yards in the time it takes you to think about it.' Faro was inclined to believe him. Very early in his acquaintance with Imogen Crowe, he had had an almost fatal encounter with a wild bull when investigating a case on the Scottish borders. He wasn't anxious to repeat that experience. At his side, Aaron sighed. 'Seems you are determined. Hold on, I'll get a rope from the stables, see what I can do. Don't move until I come back!' Waiting for Aaron, Faro looked across at the bull who looked back at him. Now aware of the two men's presence, he had stood up and was snorting but not making any threatening moves which would have brought him in direct contact with the dead man.

Aaron returned and shouted to Faro from the far side of the field where he was attempting to lasso the bull's horns with a rope. The beast didn't like that at all and, after several of Aaron's attempts, which were accompanied by angry roars, he lowered his head for the attack. It was just the action Aaron was waiting for. The rope found its target and, with a cry of triumph, he fastened the bull securely to the iron fence. He walked round the field and returned to Faro's side. Faro was amazed at his speed and his courage. 'Well done, well done!'

Aaron grinned. 'I've done all of this before, sir, many times in rodeos across the West—and been paid for it. But . . .' with a shuddering glance towards the dead man, 'never in such circumstances. At least that will keep him anchored for a while. You can go into the pen now, if you like.'

Even at that distance Faro felt a desire for instant flight but, taking faith in Aaron's rope, he climbed the fence and knelt by the remains of Mark Cara. He examined the dreadful gouging made by the bull's horns and a deep gash on his neck. One thing was immediately obvious from his many dealings with dead bodies—this was no new accident. From the evidence around the corpse, not only birds but other small animals had left their mark. The body had obviously lain in the bullpen for several days.

As he returned, Aaron asked, 'How did he come to be in the field alone? It's a bullpen, for God's sake. They've had the animal for years. Surely he knew the beast's fierce nature—that bulls are never to be trusted. Although it is unlikely that they would attack unless provoked.'

'Then provoked is probably the answer.'

Aaron frowned. 'I don't get you, sir.'

'My guess is that he did not come willingly—that someone dragged him here, drugged or disabled in some way. I think Dr Neill will uncover some interesting findings for

202

his post-mortem. A knife slash. The blood would attract the bull . . .'

'So that's how . . .' Aaron whistled and produced the horse blanket which he had also brought from the stable. 'When you're ready to go . . . Shall I?'

'If you please.'

In the manner of a toreador in the bullring, Aaron very dextrously threw the blanket over the dead man's body. 'Now let's get back. I've had more than enough.'

As they walked down the hill, he said, 'I have a theory, sir. It couldn't have been the children exacting their terrible revenge but I favour the Romanies. What do you think?' Faro had already dismissed the Romanies as a rather too obvious choice but Aaron continued, 'Physically the children could never have managed it without help but the Romanies, realising they now had only one Cara to deal with, might have seized the opportunity to take revenge.'

As they headed in the direction of the drive, Faro hesitated. 'A moment, if you please. Let us return to the house.' And, walking up the steps, he threw open the front door and asked, 'Do you not find the fact that it was unlocked interesting? Look around you. True, the dirt and squalor is hideous enough but there is no evidence to suggest struggle—no chairs or tables overturned,' he said as Aaron followed him mutely through the downstairs rooms that they had inspected earlier. They then went upstairs to the bedrooms.

'What are we looking for, sir?' Aaron asked at last, averting his eyes from the squalor.

'Bear with me, if you will, Mr McBeigh. I want you to observe that there is a great deal of valuable property untouched both upstairs and in the entrance hall. Look around you—an abundance of silver, tarnished I admit, but extremely precious and saleable, candelabra, table silver and fine paintings. Is that not so?' Aaron nodded and Faro went on, 'Do you not consider it remarkable that nowhere in the house is there any evidence of a struggle—not even an overturned chair? And I am certain that, if there was such a thing as an inventory of the contents of the house, we would find that nothing was missing. What does that suggest to you?'

Aaron frowned. 'I was thinking along the lines that Mark might have intercepted thieves —Romany thieves . . .'

'No,' Faro shook his head firmly as Aaron continued to watch him, frowning.

'I am not a detective, sir. I am not sure what you are getting at.'

Faro smiled. 'Then I will tell you. Does not the evidence or lack of evidence of violent activity suggest anything significant to you?' And, ignoring Aaron's shake of the head, he continued, 'It suggests to me that Mark Cara received a visitor that day and left the house willingly to accompany that person to the bullpen . . .'

'I see what you mean, sir.' Aaron interrupted. 'Perhaps someone came to tell him that the bull had escaped and was roaming free.'

'That is indeed one possibility. But, whatever the reason, the signs indicate that he was only intending to be gone from the house for a short time and did not trouble to secure the door.'

Aaron was still staring at him, wide-eyed behind the thick spectacles. 'What you are suggesting, sir, is . . . is . . . He stopped and shook his head in disbelief as Faro said, 'Oh, yes, there is no doubt at all in my mind that Mark Cara knew his killer. Come with me.' And, leading the way into the kitchen, he pointed to the table. 'What do you see there, Mr McBeigh?'

Aaron glanced quickly at the table and said, 'A plate of food—nothing particular about it.'

Faro laughed. 'Come now—you can do better than that. This table,' he said thumping it with his hand, 'this table contains vital evidence.'

The American continued to stare at it. Adjusting his glasses, he walked round, moved a chair out of his path and turned to Faro, shaking his head and looking increasingly baffled. 'Why, sir, it is only food—the remains of a meal . . .'

'Exactly,' said Faro triumphantly. 'A meal still on the place, the meat with a knife in it, the potatoes untouched. Does that not suggest to you that this particular meal, which he was having alone, was hastily abandoned? See, the half-empty wine glass. And that chair which you pushed back so neatly into place as you walked around is also significant.' Aaron continued to stare at him, occasionally shaking his head, as Faro insisted, 'All of this is evidence, Mr McBeigh.'

Aaron frowned. 'Evidence of . . . what, sir?'

'Evidence that Mark Cara's last meal was interrupted.' Faro pointed dramatically at the table. 'It is all there for us to see. Look at that abandoned plate—it tells us he threw down his knife, pushed back his chair and left the table in a considerable hurry to meet his visitor. That visitor was the last person to see him alive.' He then added, soberly, 'And his identity, Mr McBeigh, once we know it, will also reveal his killer.'

21

As they left the house, Aaron stared back at the door as if it might give confirmation to Faro's theory. 'Your observations are truly amazing, sir. Amazing. I am lost in admiration.'

206

Down the drive, they were met by a procession heading up the hill. In the lead was the doctor in the gig with Conn at his side. They were followed at a little distance on foot by Father McNee, Paddy and an unhappy-looking young curate who had just arrived from Cork that morning to begin his probationary period with the priest.

Dr Neill greeted Faro and said, 'A dreadful business. I can scarcely believe what I have heard—is it true?'

'It is.'

'Then, since you made the discovery, would you or perhaps . . .' Pausing, he smiled encouragingly at Aaron whose well-tanned face was showing signs of stress.

Aaron shook his head and Faro said quickly, 'Then I will come with you.' Boarding the gig, he told the doctor and Conn the details of their horrific discovery.

At the bullpen, the carrion birds had returned to resume their gruesome feast and were only thrust off with some difficulty. 'Disgusting creatures,' said the doctor. 'But, to survive, some must die. It's the law of nature.'

The Kerry bull, still tethered to the far side fence, bellowed his displeasure and gave an ineffectual tug at the rope. The doctor, about to climb into the field, paused to shudder and ask, 'Is it safe?'

'Mr McBeigh made an excellent job of anchoring him,' said Faro reassuringly but, waiting by the fence, he kept a sharp lookout in the bull's direction as he clambered over the fence. The doctor, with Conn at his heels, was followed closely by the priest who was accompanied by Joseph, the young curate, and he was carrying the requirements to say a Mass for the dead. Listening to the murmurs of their voices, none of it seemed real somehow. This was the stuff of nightmares, thought Faro, as Paddy came and stood beside him, turning his bonnet round and round in his hands, muttering little shrill birdlike cries and dancing from one foot to the next. The horror of the situation seemed well beyond him too although Faro felt that he was actually enjoying being part of such a terrible scene— unlike the young curate who had to be excused his duties to go to the hedge where he was violently sick.

The doctor's examination had not taken long. He and Conn had a few words with Father McNee and then came back to Faro who asked, 'Has he been dead for some time?'

'About fourteen hours, I would estimate,' was the doctor's cautious reply.

Faro was taken aback and said, 'I would have thought considerably more than that.'

'Oh, but then you would be mistaken, wouldn't you, Mr Faro? We doctors know our jobs, I assure you,' was the smooth reply.

'I should like you to come back with me and give your official report, sir,' Conn said to

Faro, 'since you and the American gentleman discovered the body.' Faro said he would do so, frowning towards the little group around the remains of Mark Cara.

Dr Neill interpreted that glance and said, 'A sorry situation. We cannot take him back down to the village knowing the uncertain temper of the folks there regarding the Caras. Alive or dead, it is all the same to them. Especially after the Caras' shocking behaviour towards their priest. They are superstitious as you know about the dead going to purgatory without the necessary committals.'

The solution was provided by Father McNee who called across to the doctor. 'We are ready now, Doctor.'

To Faro and Conn, Dr Neill smiled grimly. 'I will stay and oversee matters here.'

'What are you intending, sir?' asked Conn.

The doctor shook his head. 'Not I, Constable. Father McNee has decided on instant committal in the family vault with his brothers. An excellent suggestion since this appalling situation certainly will not be improved by delay.' This was increasingly obvious. The stench had everyone pressing handkerchiefs to their noses—everyone except Paddy, that is, and he climbed over the fence to offer his assistance. Smiling gently, he rolled up his sleeves and seemed totally unmoved by the horrendous task or the presence of the fierce bull. His help was sorely needed. The young curate was being sick again. He was reprimanded by the priest who was attempting to wrap the remains of Mark Cara in the horse blanket.

At this point, the doctor whispered that they would take the body briefly up to the house. 'Clean him up, you know, and prepare him for interment. Perhaps the vault will then be sealed. Carasheen will approve of that. It will mark the end of a chapter—the unholy trinity—closed forever.' Along with a lot of unanswered questions, thought Faro—like a man who had already been dead for several days being dismissed as a recent accident.

'As for the bull, he will have to be destroyed,' said Conn firmly. Faro had an idea that Aaron would have a lot to say about that.

*   *   *

As Faro walked down the hill with Conn, they were greeted on all sides by folk who had heard the news and wanted all the details. There were shouts of, 'The young divil is dead, God rot him.'

'How did he die? Who killed him?'

And, 'He will go straight to hell, that's for sure!'

Ignoring such sentiments, Conn managed a dignified response by saying, 'You will have all the details in due course. We can tell you nothing definite until we have the doctor's report.'

'He is really dead tho', is he not, Constable?' was one anxious question which raised a stillness in the little crowd.

'He is indeed,' said Conn. 'For certain.'

'No doubt about it, Constable?'

'None at all.' At that, a cheer rose from many throats. Anxious looks turned to cries of jubilation. Carasheen was free—free at last from the tyranny of the Caras. Now they could look forward to living their lives, tilling their fields and going about their daily tasks without the ever-present nagging fear of the unholy trinity riding their black horses through the village, bringing with them a tide of destruction, stealing what was not given willingly and whipping folk who got in their way. And this behaviour was always accompanied by the derisive mocking laughter that some would have cause to remember to their dying days.

Faro was glad to leave Conn to deal with the crowd that clustered around him and make his escape to the inn where Aaron had already arrived and was talking to Imogen and Tom. As Faro entered the room, Imogen rushed to his side and put her arm around him. 'Faro darling, we have been waiting for you,' she said anxiously. 'Aaron told us all about it—dreadful, dreadful. Are you all right?' Assuring her that he was, Faro did not add that he doubted whether he would be able to close off

211

the fearful scene—the sight of it in his mind's eye or the smell of it continually in his nostrils. He sighed inwardly. Dear God, he had thought he was finished with such scenes, that they had been laid aside with his retirement from the Edinburgh City Police.

Imogen continued to cling to his side, her expression concerned and tender. As if she was aware of his disturbed state of mind, she led him to the window, away from Aaron and Tom and the numerous customers who had arrived to speculate on the morning's events at Cara House. 'I seem to remember we were engaged for lunch,' she said, leaning round to kiss his cheek.

Stroking her arm, he smiled wryly, saying, 'You won't be offended if I decline, will you, my dear?' At that moment, food was furthest from his thoughts—obliterated by that recurring scene in the bullpen and the stench of death. 'I am not particularly hungry,' he added.

'You look dreadful, darling,' she whispered.

'Do I? I could do with a strong drink.'

As if he understood perfectly, Tom, who had observed their retreat from the others, came over and put down a very large whiskey on the table. Thanking him, Faro drank it gladly. Watching him drain it, Tom said, 'Another wouldn't do you any harm either, sir.' And, as he picked up the empty glass, he added, 'A terrible business up yonder, but look outside if you will, sir. You will go many a mile to find a happier place than Carasheen this day—happy accident for all of us, the young devil's folly.' So he believed or had been told that it was an accident, thought Faro, as Tom went on, 'You wouldn't be knowing, sir, but there was once a lovely herd of cows up at the house—the pride of Kerry they were. But once the old gentleman died and the young devils took over, all they kept was the bull.' He paused and shook his head. 'The bull. Can you imagine keeping a bull on his own without cows—sure, it is asking for trouble. Any farmer will tell you that. Perhaps the poor beast was like the rest of Cara, just waiting for its moment of vengeance,' he ended darkly and swept away to refill the empty glass.

Imogen smiled and said, 'That must be one of the longest speeches our usually silent Tom has ever made.' Faro thought that what he had to say raised some interesting points—none more so than the fact that Mark Cara's death was being regarded as just another accident. If it was presumed that Luke was also dead, this series of accidents had effectively wiped the unholy trinity off the face of the earth. That they deserved it Faro believed was true. But none of it quite rang true. The coincidence of the three brothers meeting accidental deaths . . . one after another . . .

Tom, returning with the whiskey, wiped the table in front of Faro and offered his

213

interpretation. 'The hand of God, that's what they are saying back at the bar there. Sure, God works in mysterious ways,' he added, piously, looking at Faro for approval. Faro nodded, thinking that he would very much like to discover the identity of the human agency that lay behind those divine hands.

As he finished his whiskey, for which Tom refused payment, he and Imogen walked out into the sunshine where some of the crowd had dispersed. If only time was not against him. He wished that he had leisure to prove that the accidents had another name—murder. But Carasheen had made up its mind. Its conscience was clear. It was an act of God and that was how it would go down in their annals—just like the thunderstorm that they believed had, to their intense satisfaction, caused the death of the youngest Cara.

And Faro knew that, in this battle of wits, he would not only be facing the real murderer but the hands and hearts of every man and woman in Carasheen would be turned against him.

United, they would protect the killer in their midst. They regarded the man or woman who had released them from the tyranny of the Caras as their saviour—it was not even beyond the bounds of possibility that they might raise funds for the erection of an appropriate monument.

22

Outside, most of the crowd had dispersed and only a few remained to welcome the return of Father McNee, beloved by all and who, they hoped, had buried for ever the last of the unholy trinity.

Leaving Imogen and heading towards the police station, Faro found Conn conscientiously entering the details of the morning's discovery in his report which he handed to Faro. It read, 'Mark Cara gored to death by bull at eight p.m. last night.' This was followed by the date which Faro decided was a curious discrepancy. It must have been obvious, even to a medical student in his first year, let alone a doctor of Neill's long experience, that the body had lain in the bullpen for considerably longer than fourteen hours before he and Aaron had made the gruesome discovery.

The other question was the complete disappearance of the gypsy children from Cara House—and why this did not seem to throw any blight on the community's present euphoria. 'Where are they now and who spirited them away?' Faro asked. 'Was that before or after the Kerry bull's attack on Mark Cara? And, most important of all, I should like to know if and how the children or the Romanies were involved.'

Conn threw down his pen and shook his head. 'My grandmother was Romany and the method of Mark Cara's death does not fit in what I have ever heard of their customs. They execute by the knife. Putting a man to death by throwing him into a bullpen is not their style at all.' Pausing, he added thoughtfully, 'And they would not have left an empty house with the contents untouched—of that you can be sure, sir. I was once inside during the old gentleman's days, when I was a little lad, and I remember rich pickings—silver and fine things. The sale of such objects would have kept the Romanies in comfort for the rest of their lives.' He sighed. 'And they would not have considered it sinful in any way. The people who had once owned the objects were dead and gone and they themselves are a poor people with few resources—except what they make by their hands or . . .' he grinned ruefully, 'occasionally steal. Sure now, they would have regarded anything saleable as their right.'

Faro signed Conn's report as witness to the discovery—Aaron had already done so—and he went in search of Imogen. Returning with her to the inn for supper, he said, 'I have asked Tom for something special since we have only two days left.'

'Anything further about the accident?' she asked.

'The murder, I think you mean, my dear,' he

216

reminded her gently.

'Surely you don't think you can find out what happened and if it really was murder in two days, Faro?'

'I certainly intend to try.'

She took his hand across the table. 'Dearest Faro, please leave it alone.'

His eyebrows rose as he looked at her. 'I never expected to hear those words from you, Imogen.'

Evading his eyes, she regarded her plate. 'Don't you see? It's all worked out for the best—for everyone.'

'Except the victims.'

'How can you waste a grain of sympathy on them! They deserved to die,' she said hotly and, at his stubborn expression, she added in a calmer tone, 'How can I make you understand, Faro darling. No one in Carasheen wants to know if anyone killed them or whether their deaths were accidental. They don't care—one way or the other, they are free at last. That is all they are interested in.' Pausing, she added, 'You have no idea what it must have been like. Even I've only heard what it was like from Maeve—the last three years have been like something out of a nightmare.' And, with a shrug, she said, 'To be honest with you, I have nothing but admiration for whoever took the steps to rid the world of such vile creatures. The only thing that surprises me is that their reign of terror lasted so long—that someone didn't summon up the courage to rid the world of them before now . . .'

'Dear Imogen,' Faro interrupted, 'I realise how you feel. These are your people and your sentiments are understandable. But you are you and I am me and I have to know.' She regarded him mutinously and he sighed. 'When I left Edinburgh, I thought such crimes and violence would be behind me forever. Instead, they seem to dog my footsteps like an evil genius, wherever I go. And sometimes I wonder if it will ever end.' Shaking his head, he went on, 'I never expected to find it in a peaceful village in County Kerry—here, with you, in Carasheen. But what has happened cannot be changed and because I am certain that these accidents were in fact murders, I cannot rest with a crime unsolved.'

He looked at her searchingly before adding earnestly, 'You can hardly be surprised—you know me well enough by now.' Imogen said nothing and he continued, 'I am damned if I will go away quietly in two days' time, saying cheery good-byes to everyone—without knowing the truth. If you love me, Imogen, try to understand me,' he added with just a little desperation in his voice. 'Walk around in my shoes and see what it feels like.'

Imogen giggled. 'Sure and I have been doing just that for several years now, Faro darling. They are much too big for me, with vast areas still unexplored.'

The food and wine had been excellent—the salmon was simply perfect. Finishing her coffee, she stood up. 'All right, my dear, if that is how you want it. You have your two days.'

Faro put a restraining hand on her arm. 'Where are you going?'

'Back to Maeve's. It's getting late and I thought you might walk me across the common.'

'Stay and finish the wine first.'

As he refilled her glass she said, 'I hope I will still be able to walk after all this.'

'If you can't then I will carry you.'

She looked at him narrowly. 'And I believe you would do just that.' As she drained the wine, she looked into its depths and then whispered, 'Damn Tom's house rules. I wish I could stay with you tonight—I do wish that.'

'And I—with all my heart.'

*   *   *

Faro slept badly that night. What short intervals of slumber came his way were tormented by evil dreams. Finally, he decided at dawn that sleep had eluded him and, from the little evidence his window afforded, it appeared that the day promised well. This was confirmed as the window at the top of the stairs revealed a perfect sunrise. He went quietly downstairs, let himself out and walked across the common. Early-morning mist had gathered around the base of the old Celtic cross so that the area had been turned into the setting for one of his nightmares—nightmares in which all the demons of Irish legend, that Imogen had ever told him about, crawled out of their uneasy resting places to haunt him with hell fires. Whenever he awoke with a start from such nightmares, sweating in terror, he realised that never, in real life, had he endured such horror as he could succumb to in evil dreams. It was as if all the terrors he had encountered and suppressed as a detective inspector, all the murderers and bloodshed, lurked in the utmost depths of his being, waiting for the chance to strike.

As he walked, he looked longingly towards the house where Imogen still slept, wishing it was not too early to call on her and ask her to accompany him. Had he done so, he would undoubtedly have earned black looks for awakening the rest of Maeve's household, especially those irrepressible small children. Looking around he decided he would again take, perhaps for the last time, that first walk they had shared together, on the hill above Carasheen, overlooking Dingle Bay, where Imogen had so many happy childhood memories. The air was clear and the sunrise had turned the sea to rose. Seated on a boulder, he took out the pocket telescope she had given him on his last birthday. Far out to sea but drawn magically close by magnification, were the dark shapes of sheep-dotted islands that were mist-wreathed against the sparkling horizon. Nearer, a school of whales arose in a vast plume of spray, blew, dived and were gone. Their places were then taken by dolphins. They dipped, darted and leapt into the air as if the beauty of the morning filled them with the sheer joy of existence. Closer still, as if aware of his presence, the inquisitive heads of some seals turned towards him while others barked dog-like on the rocks below.

He laid aside the telescope for a moment and, as he looked at the scene before him, he was taken back to his childhood days in Orkney. He remembered the strange legends of the seals and their affinity with humans. He especially thought of the seal woman who was his grandmother and who, according to his mother, had webbed fingers and toes. He had always smiled at that idea, refusing to take it seriously. But the Vikings, whose blood ran in his veins, were a different matter. Their role in his life was proclaimed by the mirror in which he shaved each morning. For they had bequeathed him his yellow hair, now tarnished with grey, his rugged bone structure, high cheekbones and his wide-set eyes. They had left their ancient sagas of heroic and often bloody deeds and had lent a shape and pattern to Orkney's destiny long before the Spanish sailors, shipwrecked from King Philip's

Armada, were swept ashore to mingle their blood strain of black hair and eyes with the native stock.

For a short while, a cloud settled across the sun, causing a brief dark curtain to fall over a scene he could have watched endlessly. Then it moved on, letting the magic of Kerry, which he was sadly in danger of losing, take him captive once again. Sitting on that boulder, at peace with the world and with a feeling of affinity that all those born on islands shared with one another, he had an awareness of times past— as if all the old legends might spring to life. At that very moment, he might raise his telescope and watch Fionn and his seven warriors rise before his eyes and, with their banners flying, ride across the hills.

It was the sound of a horse that brought him back to the present. However, it was not Fionn and his warriors but a gig heading out of Carasheen in the clear morning air on the road far below. Bringing the telescope to bear on the tiny moving object, it magnified the two travellers—a woman in a white blouse, with a parasol, and a man holding the reins, wearing a distinctive wide-brimmed hat. The man had his head turned towards the woman. Faro recognised the hat first—Aaron McBeigh. And his fellow passenger, under that oddly familiar parasol he had bought for her in the Rue de Trivoli, was none other than Imogen.

He sprang to his feet, waved frantically and

called out. But they did not hear him. He called again and again, until, at last, the gig disappeared round a bend in the road. He stood clutching the telescope. Aaron and Imogen—he looked at his watch—riding out at seven in the morning. And curiosity turned to anger. A fury of jealousy arose like gall and banished the last dregs of Kerry's magic which he had longed to share with her. He did a quick calculation and concluded that she must have already been up and about when he had passed by Maeve's house, suppressing the longing in his heart and anxious not to disturb her on any account. This could not have been a spur of the moment arrangement. All must have been carefully planned—the decision made to go off on some secret jaunt with Aaron McBeigh.

Where were they heading? He raced down the hill, carrying with him a faint hope that Imogen might have left a message for him. But he did not feel like storming into Maeve's house to question her regarding Imogen's early departure. Instead, he headed back to the inn where Tom was polishing the dining room table in readiness for breakfast. He grinned at Faro, said, 'Early risers, today, sir,' and handed him what he most wanted. 'Miss Crowe left this for you.' Faro unfolded the note. It read, 'Where were you? Have gone with A. to Derrynane House. Last chance to see it. Know you won't mind—realise you are too busy right now. In haste.' Too busy, thought Faro, as he ate his breakfast of bacon, eggs and sausage. He discovered that, despite his fears that Imogen had betrayed him, the fresh morning air had given him an appetite. Betrayed? No, conscience told him he was being unfair.

And, rereading the note before throwing it away, he realised its words touched forlorn echoes of his early life in Edinburgh, when, after Lizzie died, he was always 'too busy' to pay proper attention to his small daughters, Rose and Emily. Was this to be the ominous pattern of his association with Imogen? Although he believed she still loved him, perhaps doubts, that only she was aware of, were beginning to form like tiny clouds on their otherwise serene horizon. And, despite her assurances that Aaron did not attract her in the least, there was always Shakespeare's dangerous 'marriage of true minds' to consider—they had much in common, those two, he had to admit. Both were writers and both had links to Kerry. What if Aaron talked her into leaving him, opening up the tempting vista of that millionaire's life of luxury in America? Faro groaned. Such a thought was intolerable.

He could not imagine life without her.

23

His tea had gone cold. Beyond the windows, the clouds on Carasheen's horizons were no longer tiny puffs of thistle-down. Large, fierce and black, they swept in from the Atlantic, abolishing the sunshine, drowning those peaceful summer fields with threatening rumbles of thunder. 'Sure, we're in for a nasty day,' said Tom as Faro headed upstairs, 'If you fancy braving it, sir, there's umbrellas in the hall.' In his dingy bedroom, the change in the weather was a fitting companion for Faro's own deep depression and, as he watched the rain pouring down the window, he knew there was only one cure. He must put his wits to work on the events of the last two days and, with some logical thought, work out his next move towards tracking down the Cara boys' killer or killers.

Opening his notebook, he looked at his observations so far:

1. Luke Cara's body seen at Lough Beigh. Discovered by Dr Neill, riding back from a confinement in a thunderstorm, encountered a riderless horse. No opportunity to examine body as Luke's two brothers arrived on the scene. Dr Neill summoned Constable Conn and Mr Crowe, who were spending the

evening together, and returned to the lough. The brothers had removed Luke, dead or alive, despite Dr Neill's speculations that his neck was broken when the horse threw him or that he had drowned when he had rolled down into the lough.

Verdict: Accidental death.

(Note: Imogen and I were absent in Waterville and missed the storm completely)

2. Two days later, Matthew Cara found dead, also on the lough shore, by Conn in early hours of the morning, his horse tied to tree. Empty bottle of poteen beside him (stolen from the police station—Conn claimed he had confiscated it as illicit whiskey from Molly Donaveen earlier). Dr Neill summoned, from a game of poker with Aaron and Desmond, examined body—drunk on poteen, had choked on his own vomit. (Molly D. confirmed was drunk when he tried to call on her earlier that evening.)

Verdict: Accidental death.

3. Mark Cara found dead on the Cara estate, by Aaron and myself—gored to death by the Kerry bull.

Verdict: Accidental death?

(Note: Not satisfactory. The house was open, signs of a hasty departure and the gypsy children had disappeared. And why did Mark refuse to see Father McNee who delivered

Matthew's body to the house two days earlier?)

Faro sat back. Although Luke's death was unconfirmed at this stage, he was willing to believe it was accidental but the coincidences of the two following accidents were not acceptable to him. Irritatingly enough, he had been dead to the world himself when Matthew Cara was found—thanks to Dr Neill's pain-relieving drug after his tooth extraction. He felt, however, that the doctor's behaviour was odd—the discrepancy over his timing of Mark's death especially nagged at him. From his own experience of dealing with murder victims, Faro knew, by the state of the corpse, that it was days since death had taken place rather than the fourteen hours claimed by the doctor. He threw down his pen.

And what about the missing children? Was there a clue in the priest's strange and disagreeable reception when he went to deliver Matthew's body to his brother? There was only one obvious answer—that Mark was already dead and there existed a strong possibility that both he and Matthew had died within hours of each other, on the same night. If he could work out how these prepared 'accidents' had been skilfully engineered, Faro knew he would have a very good idea of the killer's identity—or killers' identities. Dr Neill could have been wrong about Luke being

227

dead. If this was the case and the youngest of the Cara brothers was still alive, would he have murdered the other two? Faro felt certain that whoever killed Matthew Cara had to be the same person who called at Cara House and induced Mark to rush out to the bull.

He did not have far to look for an answer as to who that might be. Aaron McBeigh was the one person with an interest in the prize Kerry bull—he was prepared to offer Mark Cara an exorbitant price. Did he go with him to the bullpen, strike him down with a blow that drew blood and push him into the field for the bull to finish off? Feeling suddenly sick at heart, Faro realised that it was essential for Aaron to have had someone to accompany him when the discovery of the body was made. And who better than Faro himself? How easy it would have been for the American to plant his own lariat across the road, trap Matthew, force him to drink the poisoned poteen and then make it look as if he had drunk himself to death. He had probably relied on Dr Neill accepting the evidence of his own eyes rather than insisting on a post-mortem which might have detected the poison. Did Aaron then leave Matthew's body and ride quickly to Cara House with an excuse—perhaps an elaborate story about seeing the Kerry bull roaming free—to lure Mark Cara to his death? Faro had a feeling of certainty that, somewhere in his speculations, lay the truth—that Aaron McBeigh was the guilty one.

His deliberations, he believed, accounted for the deaths of two of the brothers, presuming that Luke's death might still be the only accident. One important thing, alas, was still lacking—the motive. What had Aaron McBeigh to gain? But of much more concern to Faro, at that moment, was the fact that Imogen, all unknowing and alone, was spending the day with a ruthless killer.

Knowing that he was in danger of treading the path where injustice lay, Faro laid aside his pen and calmly read over his notes. He had always been aware of the trap that had been the downfall of many detectives—the trap baited with prejudice which had led them to condemn innocent men and women to the gallows because of personal detestation or ulterior motives. He knew some who had even gone to the ultimate length of planting enough evidence for a conviction. This was almost exactly what he was guilty of himself with regard to Aaron McBeigh. Here he was building up evidence primarily based on personal dislike, the human frailty of jealousy and the coincidence of the American's interest in the Kerry bull. But Aaron, from the more accessible evidence of his own eyes, was not a mean man. As a millionaire, he could afford to be lavish with money but not by the wildest stretch of imagination could Faro believe he killed Matthew and Mark Cara just to obtain

229

the Kerry bull at a bargain price.

With a sigh, Faro realised the dangers of seizing upon circumstantial evidence and decided he must open his mind to another possibility, one much closer to Carasheen— Desmond Crowe. After all, Desmond had the best motive of all—avenging his natural daughter's murder. Faro recalled that, only a short while ago, Desmond had occupied the role of prime suspect. Not only was the murdered Peg his daughter, he had lied about summoning official police reinforcements to help him investigate the Donnelly murders. The personal reasons he had given Faro, regarding his forced retirement and his anxiety to solve the case on his own, were plausible enough but they might also be a pack of lies. Had he intended to kill Carasheen's unholy trinity? Was he aware that he could rely on his friend Dr Neill not looking too closely into their deaths, especially as the village would be counting their blessings at being rid of their tormentors?

Faro went right back to the Donnelly slayings. Despite the mocking denials, defiance and threats of the Cara brothers, he was certain that it had been these two deaths that had begun it all. And the evidence of the sole witness, the simple-minded Paddy, seemed indisputable. The unlikely onset of a brainstorm in Paddy's head and the subsequent murder of the young couple to whom he was devoted seemed beyond logical contemplation. However, it was well within the bounds of possibility that Paddy could have sneaked into the police station, stolen the bottle of poteen and added poison to it—such things as arsenic were readily available in village homes and farms for the poisoning of vermin.

He could also have stolen his idol Aaron's lariat, stretched it across the road at the lough and lain in wait to trap Matthew Cara. But Faro did not believe that Paddy could have forced him to drink the poteen, thrown him down the slope to the lough and then rushed up to Cara House to lure Mark out to the bullpen by telling him that the bull had escaped or some such story. Apart from anything else, it was doubtful if Paddy could have made Mark understand a word he was saying. Faro shook his head. No, these 'accidents' were much too well thought out and planned to be laid at the threshold of a simple mind. Such tactics certainly needed considerably more physical strength and ingenuity than Paddy possessed.

It was also very unlikely, given his capacity for passionate devotion—Aaron McBeigh was a prime example—that he could have taken an axe to the young couple on their way home from the wedding. For one thing, the killer would have been covered in their blood but, when Paddy went to report what he had seen,

231

there had been no mention of this. Faro shook his head, wondering, as he considered his two suspects, how he might raise the subject tactfully with Father McNee.

Desmond had the stronger motive. Although Aaron had plenty of evidence piling up against him and was, therefore, the more likely suspect, it had to be admitted that he had no motive whatsoever. He was a visitor who had arrived in Carasheen ostensibly to discover his Kerry roots and buy a bull to take back for his ranch. But, Faro thought sourly, he could also be in pursuit of Imogen Crowe with whom he had long been infatuated. He still felt angry that the American had been keeping in touch with Imogen's movements through her publishers. And she had kept his letters to herself—perhaps wisely, Faro's conscience told him, knowing his dislike of the man.

He considered the third man to be most involved in all of this—Dr Peter Neill. Although he was quite excellent as a dental surgeon, he was incompetent as far as being able to tell the time of death correctly was concerned. And, in his eagerness to declare all three deaths as accidents, he could be an accessory to murder—either intentionally or because he was being blackmailed or through fear of the consequences to his family.

Faro wrote down the three names. Of these, Desmond had the best motive and this led him to Molly Donaveen, whom he had earlier dismissed as a physical improbability. The worst that could be said for her was also that she could be an accessory to murder. If, knowing that Desmond intended murder, she had lured his victim, Matthew Cara, to her house that night, then she was his accomplice. There was only one vital flaw—when Conn arrived to announce the discovery of Matthew Cara's body, the three men had been in one another's company playing cards all evening. Which left Conn himself. The person who discovers the murder victim is often one of the prime suspects and Conn would certainly not be the first policeman to be found to be corrupt.

But, again, there was a flaw—the lack of motive. What had Conn to gain, apart from a possible promotion, by bringing the killer of the Cara boys to justice? At the price of becoming the most unpopular man in Carasheen! But was escape from the dreary routine of Carasheen enough to make him commit two murders if his heart was set on marrying the Donaveen factor's daughter?

Or was it possible that Conn saw himself as the saviour of Carasheen, riding out to rid the village of their unholy trinity? Again, Faro shook his head. He was totally unable to visualise young Constable Conn in such a heroic role. Scoring off his name, he decided that the priest could also be left off his list.

24

Faro was having lunch in the busy inn. It was much busier than usual and he was certain that, although the talk was in the Irish, the main topic of conversation concerned the holy miracle that had rid them of their unholy trinity. Glances and an occasional smile came his way but no one came to speak to him.

Finishing his stout, he looked out of the window. The rain had stopped and he decided to call on Dr Neill with some trumped-up excuse like a sleeping draught for his travels, when he often slept badly. However, what he did not want was something with the force that had knocked him unconscious for almost two days.

Walking across the common, he met Father McNee going towards his church where Paddy was sweeping the path through the graveyard. The priest passed the time of day with him and, as Paddy looked up, smiled widely and waved to them, Faro sighed deeply. Father McNee looked at him sharply and Faro said, 'Sad that such a fine young man should have to suffer such a disability.'

'There are no such disabilities in God's eyes, Mr Faro. Paddy is as much loved by Jesus Christ—perhaps even more—than those with all their faculties. He certainly has fewer sins to answer for,' he added grimly.

Faro nodded. 'Suffer the little children—is that what you mean, Father?' The priest smiled and Faro continued, 'Witnessing that dreadful murder of the Donnellys must have been a dreadful shock but he seems to have recovered quite well.'

Father McNee looked towards the busy figure who was now weeding between the graves. 'I think, mercifully, that he has forgotten all about that terrible incident. For him, it will be no more than a bad dream would be for the rest of us.'

As Joseph, the new curate, was hastening in Paddy's direction, all fluttering cassock and determined expression, the priest continued, 'I have studied Paddy carefully during the years he has been in my charge. An interesting study, indeed—for he is a creature who lives from day to day, even sometimes, I suspect, from hour to hour. His poor brain can only cope with present events—the past soon fades into oblivion.'

Faro nodded towards the curate. 'I see you have a new helper to ease your burden a little.'

Father McNee sighed deeply. 'I fear he is to be more trouble by far than Paddy has ever been—despite having all his senses. It is quite unworthy of me, I know, but I sometimes believe God and the bishop have sent him to test my patience.' In the short silence that followed, the priest's anxious expression

235

indicated concern about Joseph and Paddy who seemed to be arguing—or, rather, the curate was doing the arguing and Paddy was smiling at him and shaking his head gently from side to side.

There was one more question Faro had to ask to finally cross Paddy off his list of suspects. 'Tell me, Father, that terrible day— when Paddy ran back to the village carrying the axe—does he not even remember being covered in blood?'

The priest stared at him. 'He certainly was not covered in blood—he had at least the sense to hold the weapon well away from his clothes. He has but few and was wearing his best shirt for the wedding.' Pausing, he gave Faro a shrewd look, knowing what Faro was getting at and, trying to put it delicately, he said, 'You have my word for it—his clothes were unmarked. If Paddy had been guilty, I would have known it. Yes, indeed, there is little in his life that he could keep from me— especially a mortal sin,' he added heavily.

Faro was about to leave with some suitable remark, when the priest held up his hand in a delaying gesture. After a moment's hesitation, Father McNee frowned and then, taking a deep breath in the manner of someone who had made a difficult decision, he said, 'There is another matter, Mr Faro, on which you could perhaps advise me. I should be greatly obliged to you, sir. I realise you are leaving soon and are doubtless very busy but, if you can spare me a few minutes only . . .'

Puzzled, Faro nodded his assent and the priest led the way down the side of the church and into the vestry. The room was little more than a large cupboard with table, two chairs and a crucifix. A row of musty black robes hung on one wall like a group of emaciated and penitent monks in a silent order. The priest indicated a chair. There was another short interval of indecision during which he scrutinised Faro carefully. Then, with a sigh and a shake of the head—as if he was still not quite sure that he was doing the right thing—he said, 'What I am about to tell you, Mr Faro, has been preying on my mind. Although I have wondered if it would be better to keep it to myself, I feel a great necessity to tell someone,' he added.

Completely baffled, Faro waited. Did his questioning look and mysterious but anxious manner concern Paddy? Was he about to hear some revelations concerning the priest's protégé that would destroy all his theories and send him back to the inn to burn all his notes on the Donnelly murder?

'When we spoke together outside just now, it occurred to me that you were the perfect person to confide in.' With a grim smile, he continued, 'Our roles are reversed, sir. Now it is I who am in the confessional because I must rely upon you to keep what I am about to divulge to yourself—to tell no one. Is that quite clear?' Without waiting for affirmation, he went on, 'You have the look and the reputation of an honest man—and there are very few of . . .'

Faro coughed gently, trying to get the priest back to the main issue. He was afraid that he was on the threshold of a preliminary and possibly lengthy sermon, complete with Biblical quotations on integrity, so he quickly said, 'I will be glad to help you if I can, Father.'

'Yes, yes. My information concerns the Cara brothers.' For an instant, Faro's spirits rose. Was it possible that the priest knew the real identify of the killers of Matthew and Mark? Father McNee's hands slid together in the attitude most natural to them—one of prayer. 'You will remember, sir, when Luke's body was reputedly taken from the lough by his two brothers, there was no official report of his death and, as the brothers were non-Christian in their beliefs or their behaviour, I was not called upon.' Pausing, he shook his head solemnly. 'I prayed for them constantly—that they would see the error of their ways and turn again to Christ's mercy but sometimes I did wonder if Luke Cara was dead at all. Was it possible that he had been merely injured in the accident when his horse threw him?'

Again Faro's spirits soared. If this was true, his own speculations that Luke Cara was still alive—and had killed his two hated brothers—

might have foundation after all. The priest continued, 'However, when I opened the burial vault to inter Mark's body, there lying on one of the shelves, cocooned in a sheet, was the corpse of his unfortunate youngest brother.' So much for that fleeting theory, thought Faro grimly. 'There was, however, another problem—a corpse that should have been there but was not. I am referring to the body of Matthew which I had abandoned in the hall in such disagreeable circumstances. The constable and I had placed it on top of a chest, presuming that Mark would place it in the vault.'

He looked at Faro, shook his head and said, 'I was shocked to realise that it was still unburied. And then I had an inspiration, I hurried back to the house with Paddy and Joseph and, lifting the lid of the chest, there was Matthew's body.' And giving Faro a bewildered glance. 'What I fail to understand is why Mark placed it in the chest instead of removing it to the burial vault alongside his brother Luke.'

'I think I may have the answer to that,' said Faro. 'I have reason to believe that Mark was already dead when you delivered Matthew's body that night.'

Father McNee nodded vigorously. 'How strange—but a quite plausible explanation. It does explain many things. Thank you, Mr Faro, for putting my mind at rest.' Faro looked at him. There were no searching questions which might have led again into the labyrinth of evidence—just calm acceptance. And the priest went on, 'Now they all lie together, the vault is resealed and a Mass has been said—although I am doubtful about the ultimate destination of their souls and I fear that all three of them will go to hell . . .'

There was a tap on the door and Joseph's anxious face poked round and indicated a crisis. Father McNee stood up and sighed. 'I am grateful to you for listening so patiently, sir. Thank God, this is the closing of a grim chapter in our lives.'

Joseph's face reappeared and the priest gave a long-suffering sigh. 'I see trouble ahead. Oh dear.' Then, smiling, he bowed, saying, 'Good day to you, sir. And, if I don't see you and Miss Crowe before you leave—the day after tomorrow, I believe—then God's blessings go with you both.'

Faro continued on his way through the village thinking of the priest's words. As for that 'grim chapter' being closed, it was not so for him. There were still many questions and precious little time remained to find the answers. Dr Neill's house was deserted so he went on to the police station where, again, he was unlucky. Wondering what to do next, the weather decided for him. The rain began once more so a walk was out of the question and he hurried back to the inn and went up to his room. Suddenly feeling unutterably weary and defeated, he lay down on the bed, intending to rest for a while. He opened his eyes some time later, feeling guilty and angry with himself for sleeping. His pocket watch said five o'clock and he had wasted a whole afternoon when he should have been continuing his search for clues.

25

Walking towards the doctor's house, Faro was hailed by Conn who was about to leave the police station. Greeting him, Faro said, 'I was hoping to see you. I was wondering if you might be persuaded to take me to the Romany camp. Seeing I can't talk their language, perhaps, with your help, we might find out what happened to those missing children.'

Conn shook his head. 'Too late, I'm afraid, sir. I went there first thing this morning—same idea as yours—to find out what happened to those children. Camp was deserted—every trace of men, women, children, animals and caravans has vanished.' He paused dramatically. 'Quite uncanny. Gave me quite a turn, I can tell you. Looked as if they have been spirited away. Apart from the scars of campfires and grass bruised with wheel marks, there was nothing—not even a piece of debris—to show that they had lived there for over a hundred years. The place looks as if it has never been occupied.'

'Which suggests, does it not, that they may have had something to do with the deaths of the Caras?' asked Faro. Conn did not seem encouraged to speculate on this. He merely frowned and Faro continued, 'Any idea where they might have gone? And how did they slip away without anyone in Carasheen being alerted?'

The constable looked blank. 'Sure, it is baffling but they could have stolen out on their own side of the lough—slipped away on the Cara estate side, invisible to the village. I don't doubt that, with a whole tribe of them on the move, we'll probably get sightings of their progress through other villages. I'll keep the local police on the lookout in the most likely places on the map.'

'They must have managed this exodus in a remarkably short while. When were you last aware of them?' Faro asked.

Conn thought for a moment. 'I spotted smoke from their fires across the lough a couple of days ago. There are many Romany sites throughout the south-west here—Kerry and Cork, for a start. They are a tight-knit community and presumably they have their own means of keeping in touch with one another. But I agree with you, certainly the speed of their departure is remarkable.' It was indeed and it suggested to Faro that their disappearance most probably dated from Mark Cara's death—that final chapter.

'There is something else you might like to see, Mr Faro,' said Conn solemnly, taking a sheet of folded paper from his pocket. 'Pushed under the door while I was away.' Printed in large letters were the words: 'I am Watchin. Do Nothing If you Value your Life and your Future Prospects. A Well wisher.'

'What do you think of that?' asked Conn.

A threatening letter and reasonably well written apart from one misspelt word which might have been accidental. It indicated to Faro that there was one person in Carasheen, at least, who was scared of the truth coming to light. Ignoring the constable's question, he asked, 'How do you intend to respond?'

Conn shrugged. 'Wasting their time, whoever it was. There's not much any of us can do now—even if we wanted to. Two murders accounted for and their killers dead by the grace of God. Divine justice, that's what I'd call it, Mr Faro, wouldn't you?'

Faro had his own views about that and they were quite unrelated to anything remotely as biblical as divine intervention. 'What will happen to Cara House now?' he asked.

'It is too early to decide but I expect the valuable contents will be auctioned in one of the big towns and the money distributed among the folks here—it will be a great help to

243

many of them. So good will come of evil, after all.'

'What about the Kerry bull?'

Conn laughed. 'Mr McBeigh can have that and welcome to it, I should think, and at a bargain price. Although I am sure he will insist that his money should go into the common good fund. I can tell you, Mr Faro, no farmer here would consider giving the animal field room. A bull that kills is very unlucky.'

Particularly for its victim, thought Faro wryly, as they parted.

His luck was in this time as he continued his way across the common. The doctor had finished his calls and his surgeries for the day and was about to sit down to supper. Pleased to produce the required sleeping powder from his dispensary, with an assurance that it was very mild, he insisted that Faro stay to supper and share Margaret's excellent soup, a ham pie and one of Faro's favourite puddings, a jam roly-poly.

The talk was of family matters. A daughter still at school, a son in his first year as a medical student, following in his father's footsteps at Dublin University and another daughter who had married a neighbouring farmer's son at seventeen and now lived in the next village. A very pretty domestic scene, thought Faro—this pleasant intelligent doctor with an attractive wife who obviously adored him. They seemed a devoted couple and he

244

had to admit that he could not imagine the Peter Neill who was his host in the role of a ruthless killer.

Magaret Neill and the shy pretty schoolgirl, who had hardly spoken a word, cleared the table and withdrew to the kitchen, leaving the two men together. 'Fancy a game of cards? Poker perhaps?' asked the doctor hopefully.

'I don't play,' Faro laughed. 'I'm a poor gambler and I've never been lucky at cards.'

The doctor grinned and winked at him. 'You know what they say—unlucky at cards, lucky in love. And judging by our lovely Miss Crowe,' he added archly. 'I think I'd prefer my luck to run that way.' Faro smiled and Dr Neill continued, 'You should have had Aaron teach you poker. He's a devil at the cards—learned all the tricks during his days in the Wild West, he tells us.' His face suddenly sad, he sighed. 'We'll certainly miss his expertise when he goes but our purses will be a little healthier. And we must look on the bright side. There are changed days ahead for our little village after our years of tyranny. Let us hope we can all live together in peace again.'

'I would be very interested to learn a little more about Sir Michael Cara—he was what we call a laird in Scotland,' said Faro.

The doctor nodded. 'A fine gentleman in spite of his English ways. All that going across to be educated and such nonsense and coming back to ape Ireland's old enemy.' He shook his head. 'But, in spite of him carrying on the tradition of landowners and overlords, which has been our misfortune for past centuries, he was very fair and very popular. No one had a bad word to say against Sir Michael. Poor gentleman, he suffered greatly after his first wife's death.'

The maid came in, curtseyed and, drawing the curtains on the setting sun, lit the lamp and stirred up the peat fire. Dr Neill indicated that they should move to the armchairs where the fire's warm glow enveloped them, casting out the room's dark shadows. Watching the maid leave, the doctor said, 'They will tell you medically that a human heart cannot break but I am sure that, one day, science will be proved wrong. For a broken heart, without hope of any cure from me, was the melancholy condition I witnessed here in Cara. When he met the English lady, everyone was so pleased for him—the whole village wished him well and it seemed to me that perhaps I had been mistaken and that particular heart was going to be mended after all. They were so happy for their short time together. No bairns, alas, to threaten the future of those three young devils. But, even so, how they hated her.' His face darkened and he looked earnestly across at Faro. 'I am telling you, sir, something I have never told a living soul.'

He paused and Faro said softly, 'You thought that they were responsible for her death.'

The doctor started guiltily. 'How did you know that?'

'Mere conjecture, Doctor, knowing the vile nature of the creatures. Please go on.'

Neill gave a great sigh and shook his head. 'I am sure they destroyed her but there was no way I could prove it. She fell out of an upstairs window—according to them, she was trying to adjust the latch. That is how it was described to me. But, oh, if you had seen Sir Michael's face, the anguish and despair—and the way he looked accusingly at his three sons, standing together, smug and smiling. That scene aroused doubts in my mind and gave me nightmares, I can tell you.'

'You believe she was pushed out of the window.'

'I do. I am certain of it and I suspect that Sir Michael was too. But he could not face the horror that his three sons might be responsible. I did not see him very regularly after that until he had the stroke that left him partially paralysed. Visiting the house, I saw it with my own eyes then—he lived in terror of his three sons. I suspect that he might have called for me earlier, during those last days, but he was restrained. Then somehow he got a note to me, delivered by his gardener—a very frightened man, gazing over his shoulder all the time, eager not to be seen at my door. The note said that he wished to see me privately as fast as I could arrange a visit.' He shook his head sadly. 'I went immediately but, by the time I got to the house, I was too late. He was lying at the foot of the stairs with his neck broken. Taken a fit and fallen, according to his sons who seemed remarkably unconcerned by this tragedy.

'As I reluctantly signed the death certificate, never believing for one moment that it was an accident, they stood over me smiling, asking about my wife and my pretty daughters. In any other family, such conversation would have been perfectly normal and polite but their eyes gleamed—a sort of terrible triumph. Then they couldn't get me out of the house quickly enough—but not forgetting to give their fondest regards to Mrs Neill and in particular to those two pretty girls. That, even to a man with little imagination, seemed to hold a hidden threat.'

He paused and looked again at Faro. 'I was scared, I have to admit it. I knew it was weak of me to sign that certificate when I suspected that old Cara had been thrown down the stairs. But I knew—as God is my witness—that, if I had made a fuss, it would be the worse for me. The threat to my dear wife and children had been made quite obvious. I was a coward, I confess, Mr Faro, but my family had to come first. Now, sometimes, knowing they are safe from the Caras, I think if only I could have brought that unholy trinity to justice then,

Carasheen might have been spared these past years of tyranny.'

It was a fearsome story of an uneasy conscience that the good doctor had lived with for years now and would continue to haunt him for the rest of his days. For Faro, it explained many things. In particular, he now understood the doctor's caution and his eagerness to describe the Cara deaths as accidents rather than face the consequence of telling the truth and dredging up the past which would destroy any doctor's plausibility and would certainly not add to his list of trusting patients.

Mrs Neill came in with tea and fruitcake. Her sunny presence destroyed the last dregs of her husband's confession and, again, the conversation reverted to normality. Dining around that pleasant table had been like a breath of fresh air in Faro's life. He enjoyed briefly witnessing a normal family life. During his long service with the Edinburgh police, he had come to know what guilt was all about and carried his own burden, despite having done his duty to the utmost of his abilities. He had guarded the community and caught criminals with the consequent neglect of his orphaned daughters.

He had now come to realise that his hopes with Imogen were being similarly blighted. He had no one to blame but himself for falling in love with an ardent feminist whose early association with Irish nationalists and her term in an English prison now barred her for ever from Britain. Thinking of Imogen at that moment was a sharp reminder, a sickening blow in the pit of his stomach, of what she had been doing. While he had been, as she put it, 'too busy' tracking down clues as to how the Cara boys had died, she had spent the day with Aaron McBeigh.

A melodious clock in the hall struck ten o'clock. Thanking the Neills for their warm hospitality, Faro made his excuses and bade them a hasty goodnight. Imogen should be home by now.

26

There was a bright moon to light his way across the common. What a stroke of luck, he thought, as he noticed a lamp still burned in Maeve's parlour window. She had not yet retired and was doubtless sitting by the fire talking to Imogen who would be telling her of the day's events. As he reached the front door, it opened. 'I thought it was you coming up the path, Jeremy. Is there something I can do for you?'

'Imogen?' The word was a question.

Maeve looked baffled and shook her head. 'She isn't back yet.' And, glancing at the darkening expression on his face, her surprise turned to embarrassment. 'I expect she got delayed,' she said soothingly and then, with a twinge of anxiety, she added, 'I do hope she's all right. It has been a very long day for her— away practically at the crack of dawn, like that, without having a proper breakfast in her either . . .'

But Faro was no longer listening. He did not need to, she was voicing all the fears in his own heart. He bid Maeve goodnight and told her not to worry. He assured her that Imogen could take good care of herself and that there would, no doubt, be a simple explanation. And, unconvinced by his own comforting words, he set off for the inn. Could Imogen take care of herself? Did this token of her failure to return from the outing to Derrynane House put the cap on his worst fears? As he crawled into his lonely bed, he decided that he had lost her forever. The visit to Kerry and Carasheen which had promised so much had robbed him of the woman who was most dear to him in the whole world—Imogen Crowe.

Sleepless, he now saw the Irish visit not as a mere holiday but the building up of a crisis in their lives together. The victim of his own remarkable memory, he went over every tiny detail, every small argument or clash of wills. The pillow beside him would forever remain empty. Somewhere between Carasheen and Waterville, Imogen and Aaron were spending the night together. At this moment, she was in his arms. He was making love to her . . .

The visions were so terrible, so unendurable, that he sprang out of bed and, lighting the lamp, he took out the notes he had written earlier in the day and to them he added Dr Neill's revelations about the Cara family. It was a monstrous catalogue. He now believed that his suspicions about the unholy trinity, as they became known, had been confirmed—they had indeed started their vile murderous activities at an early age and were responsible for the death of their young stepmother and their father.

The hours ticked by and he was still at work. With only one more day left, he went carefully over every word he had written, fully realising, in his own heart, that he was naming Aaron McBeigh as the prime suspect. Not because the evidence was stronger against him than it was against Desmond, who at least had a strong motive, but because he had never liked the American, his rival for Imogen Crowe. If only he could find sufficient motive to pin the murders on Aaron. The main trouble was that Aaron and the doctor and Desmond all had alibis. For a detective like himself, that was a stumbling block and his other severe handicap was not having been present to examine the evidence at the crime scenes, where the murder of the Donnellys and the subsequent so-called accidents to the Cara boys had taken place. He had a sudden realisation of what he had overlooked. All at once, he knew exactly what had happened. He threw down his pen with a laugh of triumph. The truth was like a blinding light . . . Except that the blinding light was real and it came from outside.

Below his bedroom, the inn was stirring, doors were closing, people were shouting. He heard calls of, 'Fire, fire!' and he rushed to the door where he was met by Tom's startled face. 'I was just coming to tell you, sir, Cara House is on fire . . .'

Dressing hastily, Faro ran out of the inn to join the stream of people heading up the hill to the most magnificent bonfire ever to be seen in the history of Carasheen. The house on the hill was enveloped in an aura of fire and flames leapt into the sky as they licked the roof and chimneys. As Faro ran towards the blaze, he saw faces he knew—Conn, Dr Neill and Desmond—and, although they possessed gigs, they had not waited to harness horses but were racing ahead on foot. Many were strangers to him for it seemed that the whole of Carasheen was heading up to the fire. The beacon must have been visible for miles around.

By the time he reached the drive, some had already visited the burning house and were rushing past him, down towards the village, clutching pictures, chairs and small pieces of furniture, clocks and candlesticks. They were exclaiming excitedly to one another. 'Anything left?' someone called.

'Fine pickings—plenty for all!' was the response as, behind him, Faro heard the rumble of farm carts. At last, he stood on the lawn, facing the house. He watched the villagers emerging from the right wing which was not yet ablaze. From somewhere there came a monstrous thunder as part of a roof collapsed and sent a pillar of flame shooting upwards. People continued to rush past him, laughing to one another as they proudly brandished their trophies. No one was attempting to put out the blaze. They would have been hard put to find water enough and the house would soon be a charred ruin. The village was taking its revenge for the tyranny it had suffered and amongst their haul some mementoes were valuable, some valueless.

Conn came to his side. He too was smiling. 'They might have waited for that auction—it would have brought them more than this.'

'You think it was deliberate?'

Conn stared at him as if he was mad, shrugged and asked, 'What else?' What a waste, thought Faro, as Conn said, 'I imagine that they wanted to make certain sure they had seen the last of the Caras.'

He sounded remarkably unconcerned, thought Faro, as shouts from nearer the scorching flames had him rushing forward. 'What is it?' cried Faro.

'Seems they think they saw someone—in the

254

house.' Conn shouted over his shoulder and Faro followed him, reacting without thinking to the natural instinct to rescue another human being from the inferno. But then they saw it was only one of the statues that had fallen against a window. 'Just as well she's made of marble, no human could have survived that,' said Conn and he disappeared into the crowd.

Faro moved well away from the fire and stood on the lawn by an old elm which seemed to shiver as if in terror. There was nothing he could do but watch that unending tide of people who seemed, from the distance, to be as small as ants as they carry away their booty. Suddenly he heard a voice nearby. 'Faro—where's Faro? Oh dear God . . .' A sob. The voice was familiar and the figure who emerged into the light was Imogen. She saw him and threw herself into his arms. 'Oh thank God, thank God! Someone told me they'd seen you rushing into the house—something about gypsy children.' Moaning as she spoke, Imogen clung to him, kissing his cheek. 'Oh dearest, dearest Faro—I thought I had lost you.'

Assuring her that he was fine and that the house was empty, he said, 'There's nothing we can do here. Shall we go?'

She nodded mutely. 'I heard all about it on the way up. I ran all the way. They were all telling me to hurry while there were pickings left.' As they were leaving, there was a final thundering sound and they looked back to see the remaining wing of the house collapse in a cloud of flame. It was the wing that contained the old chapel and the family vault so the destruction of the Caras was now complete. Even the bones of their generations, the old coffins and effigies had vanished forever into a scene from Dante's 'Inferno'.

They reached the common and, as they walked past the inn, Imogen asked, 'Where are you taking me?'

'To Maeve's, of course. Isn't that what you want?'

She eyed him narrowly. 'No, it damned well isn't, Jeremy Faro. I'm not leaving you tonight. I'm staying with you, even if we have to sleep under a hedgerow.' And, so saying, she marched towards the open door of the inn. She turned to him and said, 'I remember which is your room. Correct me if I'm wrong.' Once inside, she closed the door. The lamp was still lit and the room looked grey in the predawn light.

Looking at him, she said softly, 'Are you waiting for something? Are you too tired perhaps?' In answer he took her in his arms, his embrace convincing her that he was certainly not too tired. He led her towards the bed and, as they undressed, she said, 'I have a lot to tell you.'

In answer, he placed his fingers over her lips and feeling her soft flesh in his arms, he said,

'Nothing that cannot wait until morning when we will both have a lot of explaining—in particular to Tom, I fancy,' he added wryly.

From the depths of his arms she laughed, saying, 'But meanwhile we have a few precious hours—that are all our very own.'

*   *   *

All passion spent, they slept well into the morning. Normal life of the inn had been resumed and they were awakened by the maid knocking at the door after she had found the key had been turned in the lock. Opening the door cautiously so as not to disturb the still sleeping Imogen, Faro took in the ewer of warm water and began his morning ablutions. At last he was aware of her face in his mirror. She was sitting up in bed and looking very pleased with herself. They exchanged the conventional remarks about having slept well and then he said, 'You were going to tell me something last night—an explanation of some kind.' She looked at him, frowning slightly, as he said, 'Go ahead—I can listen to you while I'm shaving.'

She watched him soaping his face and taking up the razor. Sitting up and clutching her knees, she said, 'I don't know where to begin. I presume you got my note.' He nodded and she said, 'We had a very pleasant day in Derrynane. It was Aaron's last chance—and mine too . . .'

Turning slightly, he said, 'You can spare me the details if they are painful.' As she scowled at him, he smiled. 'What I am really interested in is last night and what delayed your return. What kept you both so long in Waterville or wherever you went to after the O'Connell house?'

She shrugged. 'You have got it all wrong, Faro. Aaron wasn't with me—I returned here alone last night and left him in that splendid hotel where we all had lunch—remember?'

'I do indeed. But surely it did not take you eight hours to get back?'

'Will you listen—for once,' she demanded impatiently. 'After Derrynane, which was splendid and very useful for my book, we went to Waterville where Aaron was hoping to complete his research into his family roots. On the way we had a slight accident with the gig— ran off the road taking a corner too sharply and damaged a wheel. It was then five o'clock. We limped into Waterville and Aaron took the gig to the carriage makers' whilst I went to the hotel to wait for him. He came back with the news that they could not provide a new wheel until tomorrow so it looked as if we would need to stay overnight. He said he had booked us into the hotel and asked if that was all right with me.' Pausing, she looked at Faro as if expecting an interruption but there was none. 'I said no, it was not all right and that I was not

258

to be compromised by staying in Waterville overnight with him. He seemed surprised, tried to persuade me that you would not mind when you knew the circumstances.'

She laughed, wide-eyed. 'I realised he had not the slightest idea of what you were like— or that, had I been your wife officially, this would have been, what your lawyers so quaintly call, a case of criminal conversation or adultery. At first I thought he was just naive then, making an excuse to leave him, I looked in the register and found that he had booked us into a double room. I was simply furious. He blustered and said there was only one room available—there was a wedding in the hotel—and that he was prepared to sleep on the sofa. I said that would not do at all and that I was determined to make my way back to Carasheen that night. I had not the least idea how I was to do this. I was certain of only one thing—that we were to be nowhere near each other, not even in the same village that night. Then, by a stroke of fortune, as I rushed out of the hotel, a crowd of young guests from the wedding were leaving. They asked me if I wanted a lift somewhere and it turned out that they were heading back to Tralee. That must have been about ten o'clock. I was grateful until I realised how long this journey was going to take. There were ten of them—boys and girls, all very young—and each one, it seemed, had to be deposited at his or her own farm or village on the way back. And, at each place, there was an invitation to come inside and have a jar, with the result that we did not even get as far as Carasheen, with two couples still to go to Tralee, until the early hours of this morning. And what greeted me? An inferno at the Cara's house. Everyone away to it and you know the rest.'

Drying his face, Faro went over and sat on the bed beside her, took her hands and kissed them. 'I hope you are pleased by my virtuous response to Aaron McBeigh's intentions. I can tell you during that very uncomfortable ride on the farm cart, there were times when visions of a soft bed . . .'

She laughed and Faro said, 'Which you did have—eventually.'

'As a reward for virtue?'

Faro shook his head. 'No, because you love me and I love you and nothing outside—only ourselves—can change that.'

Imogen nodded. 'I did a lot of thinking on that journey last night. Looking at those young people, not one of them more than seventeen or eighteen, so happy and carefree. What was time to them? And I thought of myself at their age. At seventeen I was in prison and my whole life since has been devoted to lost causes—aye, Faro, believe me, they are lost indeed. And, with them, went my youth, twenty years when I should have married and had children—when I should, had God been willing, have met you. By the time we did meet five—six—years ago it was already too late for me.'

'It was never too late, Imogen—and it isn't too late now. We can marry . . .'

'But I cannot bear you a child so what's the point? We are both too old for that and too restless and ambitious to settle down into carpet slippers and muffins by the fire.' Imogen swung her legs out of the bed and said, 'Talking of restless ambition and explanations, I had best think of something that sounds convincing for Maeve—although,' she paused, smiling at him as she dressed, 'I have a feeling that she knows perfectly well. As we are leaving very soon, I must pack.'

'I'll pick up your luggage, leave it here and we'll get it on the way to the railway station.'

'Splendid—what about you?'

'Things to do. Lines to draw under inconclusive evidence.' Faro sighed. 'I've been through it all, looked at all the suspects . . .'

'Like who?' she said, attempting to comb the tangles from her hair.

Faro drew a deep breath. 'Your uncle Desmond is the only one who seems to have a credible motive.'

'I cannot believe that of him. You will never convince me.

'My other suspect, your friend Aaron, has no motive for murder.' Imogen looked up, seemed about to say something and then

261

shook her head.

As he was buttoning up his shirt, she wandered across to the table and picked up the small white packet Dr Neill had given him. 'And what is this for? Are you ill? Is there something you haven't told me?' she added in alarm.

About to put on his boots, Faro laughed. 'Of course not. Merely an excuse to talk to the good doctor. Told him I had problems sleeping when we travelled.'

Imogen held the packet in her hand, with a distasteful expression. 'A sleeping draught. Sure now, let's hope it isn't as effective as the last one he gave you. I don't want a Rip Van Winkle . . .'

Faro threw down the shoehorn and sprang to his feet. 'Say that again!' he exploded.

'Wh . . . what? I only called you a Rip Van Winkle!'

He rushed across to her. 'That's it! That's it!'

'Faro! What on earth are you talking about?'

'You, my darling girl, have solved it.'

27

Brandishing his notes, he said to Imogen, 'Last night, I couldn't sleep—for obvious reasons—and I was just seeing, at last, what the answer was to two of those three accidents—murders—yes, that's what they were—when Cara House went on fire.'

'Then perhaps you will let me into the secret,' said Imogen.

Faro sat down on the bed beside her. 'Yes, I think I can do exactly that. It was all so easy. I had it all the time—kept coming back to it. The thing that kept troubling me was the fact that it couldn't be your uncle Des or Aaron or the doctor because, when Conn came to tell them about Matthew, they had been together all evening playing poker.'

'So . . .'

'Don't you see it now? The answer is that Matthew didn't have one killer—he had three. The doctor, Aaron and Uncle Des all provided each other with alibis in the form of Aaron's extended poker game.' Imogen didn't look convinced and he went on. 'Let us say that Luke's death was an accident. He was drunk and the horse took fright and threw him. But I think that accident planted the idea. Desmond knew . . .'

'Oh, so you're trying to blame Uncle

Desmond, are you?' Imogen cut in shortly.

Faro raised a hand. 'Hear me out, if you please. Molly had told Desmond that the three young hooligans were all courting her. They were determined to wear her down, intimidate her or blackmail her into signing a marriage bond with one of them and so turn over all her property. So they were travelling most nights on the road by the lough. There was only one small problem. Your uncle was an ex-policeman and, once a detective always a detective, he had already sought my help to solve the Donnellys' murders. He guessed—rightly—that I would be very interested in anything that happened to the Cara boys.'

Pausing, he thought for a moment. 'So I had to be got out of the way, while they were thinking about it, and my toothache gave them the perfect answer. Dr Neill extracted the tooth and drugged me so powerfully to kill the pain that I slept for more than twenty-four hours. While I was dead to the world, the doctor added poison to the bottle of poteen Desmond had stolen from Conn. They set up the trap for Matthew with Aaron's lariat . . .'

'Wait a moment, Faro. How did they know he or his brother would be going to Donaveen so conveniently that night?'

Faro smiled and wagged a finger at her. 'This, I think, is where an accessory to their plan was needed—one who could be trusted to lure the Cara boys to Donaveen, with an invitation they could not afford to refuse.'

'Molly, you mean?'

'Exactly. So the trap was set and all they had to do was wait. Matthew came along, riding furiously after having been turned from Molly's door. His horse tripped over the lariat, they picked him up, forced the poteen down his throat and then rolled him down to the shore of the lough. There, some hours later, another regular traveller to Donaveen— namely Conn who was courting the factor's daughter—would be sure to spot the horse tied to the tree.'

'Quite ingenious,' said Imogen, sounding unconvinced still, 'but what about Mark?'

'Ah, yes, while all this was going on at the lough, Aaron speedily took his departure and rode up to Cara House. In a very genial mood, he told Mark that he was leaving in a couple of days and asked if they could negotiate the sale of the Kerry bull. Believing that Matthew was away to Donaveen and through his usual drunken haze, Mark probably realised that he could make a deal with the American and keep all the money himself. So they walk over to the bullpen and, while Mark has his back turned, Aaron knocks him out, draws blood, tips him over the fence and leaves the bull to complete his task.' He paused. 'And where were the gypsy children all this time?'

'Keeping well out of sight,' said Imogen, 'I imagine their masters in drunken mood were to be avoided at all costs.'

Faro shook his head. 'Has something quite significant that happened afterwards not occurred to you?'

Imogen thought for a moment. 'Sure, when the priest went up to the house with his brother's body, Mark refused to see him—according to the children. That seemed odd.' Frowning, she added slowly, 'Now I understand what you're getting at. Mark was already dead, lying in the bullpen. But how can you be sure of that?'

Faro steepled his fingers together thoughtfully. 'Because he had been dead for quite some time, a day or two at least, when Aaron called on me and suggested we go up to the house together where he wanted moral support while he was negotiating the sale of the Kerry bull.'

'Aaron again?' mocked Imogen. 'How could you know how long Mark had been dead? Dr Neill said . . .'

Ignoring her interruption, Faro continued, 'Dr Neill's examination was cursory, to say the least. He was used to giving false diagnoses—he had already declared that Matthew Cara had died because he had drunk too much and had choked on his own vomit.'

'Sounds plausible enough to me.'

'Let me say that I am not used, through many years of police work, to accepting plausibility—I have to examine evidence for myself. And, in my long career, maybe I have seen many more corpses, that have lain undiscovered for several days, than Dr Neill has in his.'

'So the doctor, well respected and loved by all, is also a crook?'

'No, merely an accessory. Mark was, to put it mildly, not a fresh corpse. And Dr Neill was only doing what he had done for many years while the Cara boys' father was alive. Signing certificates regarding the accidents to their stepmother and also to their father, when he was certain the former had been murdered and Sir Michael was pushed down the stairs that killed him.'

Imogen's eyes widened. 'Let me tell you a story then.' And Faro proceeded to tell her of his interview with Dr Neill, on the trumped-up excuse of a sleeping draught, and how the doctor had confided his fears in him.

'Poor Dr Neill,' she said. 'What a terrible predicament.'

'I agree. Your compassion is quite understandable and so are his reasons for issuing false death certificates for the Cara brothers.'

Imogen looked at him. 'Presuming you are right about all this,' she said, 'where do we go from here?'

'I haven't worked that out yet.'

'We have just over an hour left before we catch that Dublin train so you'll have to look sharp about it.' At Faro's exclamation of annoyance, she smiled. 'Problem is you have no real proof, have you?' He sighed and shook his head. 'You could always go across and take the wind out of their sails—so to speak—by accusing them. You might even get a confession if they were scared enough.' Still Faro did not answer and she took his hands. 'I realise, knowing you, that this is all for your own personal satisfaction. And, if you would like to take my advice, I would say that you should regard this as one of Inspector Faro's few unsolved murder cases.'

His head jerked sharply upright and he demanded, 'And why should I do that, pray?'

She patted his hands. 'Because, dear love, you are on the road to nowhere.'

'I don't understand.'

She shook her head. 'But then, you don't understand the people of Carasheen—all they have suffered through the years. They don't give a tinker's curse, to put it mildly, what happens to whoever rid them of the Cara brothers. If it was Uncle Desmond, the doctor and the American visitor, they would be quite likely to put up a statue to all three of them on the common and venerate it like the old Celtic cross.' Pausing, she added, 'Don't you see what I'm getting at, sweetheart? Carasheen has been liberated. They are eager to bury the past and get on with their lives and, if you try to accuse them . . .' she added gravely, poking a

268

finger at his chest, 'then you, I fear, may be the next victim. Now, shall we go down to breakfast? Show our shamed countenances to Tom and the world?'

Tom took their appearance with remarkable aplomb. Maybe, unaware that the maid had found the bedroom door locked, he was prepared to assume that Miss Crowe had merely arrived just in time for breakfast. As they ate their porridge and their bacon and eggs, Imogen asked idly, 'What shall we do with our last hours before we leave? Have you anything special in mind?'

Noting his preoccupation and guessing where it lay, she said, 'I have promised to see Uncle Desmond. Perhaps you should confront him with your . . . evidence. What do you say to that?'

Faro smiled. 'I will certainly come with you but, as for confrontation, I'm not too sure . . .'

'It's now or never,' was Imogen's cheerful response.

*　　　*　　　*

Desmond was expecting them. Aaron and Dr Neill had also arrived to say goodbye. A poker game was spread out on the table. Kissing Imogen's cheek, Desmond said sadly, 'We will miss you.'

Shaking hands with Faro, Dr Neill said, 'You arrived at a trying time. Now that is all over, the Caras have gone at last.'

'Indeed,' said Faro, 'but their killer remains at large.'

Three startled faces turned towards him and Imogen said, 'Faro has something to say to you. Go on, tell them what you have just told me,' she added firmly.

Faro drew a deep breath. 'I am willing to accept that Luke Cara's death was an accident but I believe I know who killed his brothers.'

There was an uneasy laugh from Dr Neill and he said, 'My dear fellow, can you not accept a doctor's word on that before you leave? Everyone knows they were accidents.'

Faro shook his head. 'Not accidents, Doctor. Murders. Shall I tell you how I arrived at these conclusions?'

The doctor smiled confidently. 'Please do.'

Faro reiterated what he had said earlier to Imogen. During the solemn confrontation, the three men watched him and he took careful note of their expression. Sometimes a gasp or a quick nervous glance exchanged between the three men restored his confidence and told him triumphantly that he was on the right track.

At the end, Dr Neill asked, 'You really believe that Aaron did the killings?' Aaron gave the doctor a startled look as he continued, 'And that we provided him with alibis?'

'I had the word "accessories" in mind,' Faro put in.

'How extraordinary,' said Desmond. 'As you have proved to us, I have to admit that your conclusions are all very plausible but there is one serious omission—Aaron has no motive.'

There was a short silence that was broken by Imogen. 'I have a piece of interesting information for you from my visit to Derrynane yesterday.' And, with an apologetic glance in Faro's direction, she said, 'An unexpected piece of information came my way—the missing piece that completes a puzzle. Just like Faro, Uncle Des and Dr Neill, are confident that Aaron is the only one of the three of you without a motive for killing off the Cara brothers. But it just happens that he has the best motive of all.' Turning to Aaron, she asked gently, 'Don't you think you should tell them?'

Aaron shrugged. 'Why not? When we were in Waterville, I found the documents I've been searching for. They proved that my grandmother was first cousin to Sir Michael Cara's father. She went to America after the Famine but, with all the family now disposed of, I guess I would have an excellent claim to the Carasheen inheritance.' Looks of surprise were exchanged and there followed an uncomfortable pause. Were congratulations or accusations in order?

Dr Neill came up with the answer. 'A motive, alas, but not long to enjoy the benefits.'

Aaron jumped to his feet. 'No, Peter, I

forbid it. Please—I beg you . . .'

'Sit down, Aaron, and preserve your strength.' And, leaning over him, the doctor continued, 'You must tell them, Aaron . . .' and, with a despairing glance in Imogen's direction, he said, 'You surely would not wish Miss Crowe . . .'

'She was the last one I ever wanted to find out. Dammit, Peter, why couldn't you keep it to yourself? I thought that was the rule for doctors.'

While he spoke, Dr Neill produced a paper from his pocket and waved it in front of them. 'Aaron was in Dublin on his way out to Carasheen. He was in hospital for a few days. And this telegraph is the result. It reads: "Grave news. Condition fatal. Expect weeks only."' Pausing for a moment, he went on, 'Aaron is dying. He was shot in the chest, in a fight before he left America. The bullet lodged too near his heart to be removed. However, it is gradually moving closer and one day, very soon, the result will be fatal . . .'

'All right,' said Aaron. 'All I want now—all I have ever wanted is to die in Ireland and, when I came to Carasheen, I saw something—as an old lawman—I could do for the land of my ancestors. Hell, I had nothing to lose.' Turning to Faro, he said, 'You were right, I guess. It was Luke's accident that gave me the idea and these two gentlemen were my assistants. And we got away with it, Mr Faro,

272

in spite of your interfering and prying into what did not concern you. You should have left it alone. You could never win—you never had a winning card in your hand. If you did, then you couldn't play it. The Caras are dead and all that remains for me is to have my greatest wish granted—to die in Ireland.' To Imogen, he smiled wryly. 'I guess I did not want you to know any of this. I never had your love but I sure as hell didn't want your pity.'

A clock struck in the hall. Desmond stood up and said, 'Now you must go or you'll miss your train. We'll see you to the station.'

Faro held up his hand. 'No, please, none of you.' And indicating the pack of cards on the table. 'Stay and finish your game.' Imogen went over, kissed Aaron's cheek and gave him a whispered farewell.

Faro stepped forward and grasped his hand. 'You are a brave man, Aaron McBeigh. I salute you.'

Armed with their luggage from the inn, they raced towards the station as the train came steaming along the platform. It was on time and they took their seats in an empty compartment. Silently, Imogen stared out of the window for the last glimpse of Kerry. Then, with a sigh, she leaned her head against Faro and he put an arm around her.

Later they would talk but, for now, there was no need for words.